C.K.KELLY MARTIN

Canada Council **Conseil des Arts**
for the Arts **du Canada**

ONTARIO ARTS COUNCIL
CONSEIL DES ARTS DE L'ONTARIO
an Ontario government agency
un organisme du gouvernement de l'Ontario

Canadian   Patrimoine
Heritage   canadien

The publisher gratefully acknowledges the support of the Canada Council for the
Arts and the Ontario Arts Council for its publishing program. We acknowledge
the financial support of the Government of Canada through the Canada Book
Fund (CBF) for our publishing activities, and the Government of Ontario through
the Ontario Media Development Corporation, an agency of the Ontario Ministry
of Culture, and the Ontario Book Publishing Tax Credit Program.

LIBRARY AND ARCHIVES CANADA CATALOGUING IN PUBLICATION

Martin, C. K. Kelly, author
Stricken / C.K. Kelly Martin.

Issued in print and electronic formats.
ISBN 978-1-77086-502-0 (softcover).— ISBN 978-1-77086-503-7 (HTML)

1. Title.

PS8626.A76922S77 2017   JC813'.6   C2017-904447-8
                                              C2017-904448-6

United States Library of Congress Control Number: 2017945946

Cover: Nick Craine
Interior text design: Tannice Goddard, bookstopress.com

Printed and bound in Canada.
Manufactured by Friesens in Altona, Manitoba, Canada in October, 2017.

DANCING CAT BOOKS
An imprint of Cormorant Books Inc.
10 ST. MARY STREET, SUITE 615, TORONTO, ONTARIO, M4Y 1P9
www.dancingcatbooks.com
www.cormorantbooks.com

For Holly and Luke
(and Hannah, when is she old enough)

ONE

WHEN IT STARTED.

When it first started, I didn't know anything was starting. I figured it would just be a regular summer like the ones before it. But it's not. It's anything *except* regular, and now that I know that, I'm going back to write everything down, starting from the very beginning, in case something happens to me. In case later I don't remember it all.

When my friend Taneisha's parents got separated, the family therapist they saw asked Taneisha to keep a journal of her thoughts and feelings. The therapist said it could help. I really hope so. I'm counting on it.

DAY ONE

One of the funny things about staying in a house that isn't yours is the noises. You're not used to the creaking sounds, the electronic whirring of appliances, or the weird random settling din the house makes, sort of like an old man's knees cracking when he bends to slip on his shoes. At my house back in Kingston, I didn't even notice those types of things anymore — they were so familiar that I'd stopped hearing them.

That always happened eventually in my grandparents'

house in Dublin, too. I'd adjust to the house's groans and whispers and then never think twice about them. Not until the following July, when I'd have to get used to the night-time noises of my grandparents' house afresh. This was my fourth July in Ireland in a row, so you'd think maybe I'd have been over the newness of them already. I wished I *were*, because I was so tired that I had a claustrophobic feeling behind my eyes that I knew would turn into a head-ache if I didn't sleep soon.

I ignored the sensation and stared up at the ceiling in the dark, thinking about the summer ahead of me. Usually we only stayed in Ireland for a month, but my uncles were coming from Australia for a visit near the end of July, so this time Mom and I would be here for the entire summer. Dad had to look after the café he'd opened with my aunt in April and would only be able to make it over for two weeks in mid-August.

Because we spent every July in Dublin, my time in Ireland felt sort of like another life. One with a different house and different friends. But even those differences felt almost normal to me; at the start of this visit, the only thing that was unusual was that my gran repeated herself more and would ask questions I'd already answered, some-times even just a minute later. She'd been doing that over FaceTime for months too, but not so much last summer or any of the summers before. My mom said Gran had Alzheimer's disease and that her memory would slowly get worse and worse, so we had to be very patient with her. I didn't mind answering questions more than once, or even twenty times; I just wanted Gran to be okay.

Her voice was the thing that woke me up that first July night at my grandparents' house. The nightstand clock radio read almost two o'clock, and I heard her say something through the wall. My granddad's voice leaked through the drywall too, loud and surprised. Then I realized it wasn't any voice that had woken me. It was squealing from the street, like how a train sometimes sounds pulling into a station, only five times louder. I stumbled to the window to look for the source of the noise.

The street was dark and full of shadows. It had gone so quiet that I almost wondered if I'd dreamt the commotion. Suddenly, an old woman in a long fur coat careened down the street waving a frying pan. She stopped and whirled around on the pavement, her eyes searching the air and her mouth firing out words with the speed of a machine gun.

I watched the woman advance again, shuffling along the middle of the roadway. Even Irish summers were too warm for the coat she was wearing, and her feet were bare. It made me glad the street was bone dry. "Show yourself!" she roared, her eyes darting from place to place. "I know you're out there."

But if there was something out there in the dark with her, it was sticking to the shadows and biting its tongue. Meanwhile, lights flicked on inside a handful of houses; I wasn't the only one watching her. In the distance, a man stepped onto his front stoop and called something to the woman that I couldn't quite hear.

She ignored the man, clutching tighter to her frying pan as she stared up at me through my second-storey window. I shivered and stepped back. None of this felt right. The woman had begun to chant the words of a poem. Something about stars running away and shadows eating the moon. Inching back to the window after a few seconds, I ventured another glance at the street, the woman's singsong words wriggling into my ears.

If she'd seen something threatening, how would any poem help? It didn't make sense. I was about to go wake my mom when my grandfather stalked into the road. He bent his head close to the woman and laid one of his hands on her shoulder, like he was trying to calm her down. Granddad was good with people, whether they were babies, teenagers, old folks, or what, and I figured he'd have her quiet and relaxed in no time.

But I was wrong.

The old woman swung the frying pan at his chest. If she were any younger she'd probably have managed to hit him. Instead Granddad hopped back, only for a second, and then he clasped her wrist, effortlessly wrestling the frying pan from her grip.

My gran jogged into my line of vision; I'd never seen her walk so fast. Granddad was holding the frying pan while Gran stared steadily into the eyes of the woman in the fur coat, whispering something to her that made the woman nod. Her fur-covered shoulders quivered. Then the woman allowed my gran to lay a hand on her shoulder the way she hadn't let my granddad. The three of them turned and began making their way up the street, away from my spot at the window.

With everything back under control, I crawled under the covers again and — temporarily forgetting all about the jumble of strange house noises — slept straight through to morning.

DAY TWO

The next person I laid eyes on was my mother, leaning against the kitchen counter holding a cup of tea to her lips. She smiled when she saw me lope into the kitchen in the sweatpants and T-shirt I'd worn to bed. "Morning, Naomi."

"Morning." I swallowed my yawn. "Did you see Gran and Granddad and the woman in the street last night?"

Mom nodded, her head tilted to one side. "Deirdre Redmond from up the road. Your gran and granddad say she's always been sharp as a tack. They don't know what's the matter with her. Maybe a side effect of some medication, or dehydration — either can do odd things to a person. Anyway, her daughter's driven up from Enniscorthy to take her to the doctor. Hopefully they'll be able to figure out what's going on."

"Could she have what Gran has?" My mind had begun to race. "What about the noise beforehand? Mrs. Redmond thought there was something out there with her."

The line between Mom's eyes deepened. "What your gran has progresses slowly. There are other types of dementia that are fast moving, but as far as Mrs. Redmond goes, we just don't know yet." Mom set her tea down on the counter. "Except that there was nothing out there with her, okay? So don't worry about that."

"But Gran and Granddad heard the noise too," I insisted. "It was so loud that it woke me up."

Mom seemed doubtful. "I didn't hear anything. Maybe

it was a lorry out on the main road. Sound really carries at night when there's nothing to mask it."

A lorry is what people in the UK and Ireland call a big truck. Whenever Mom got back to Ireland her vocabulary slipped from North American back to Irish. But the squealing hadn't sounded anything like a truck.

"Maybe," I said. The noise definitely hadn't been Mrs. Redmond either, so what else could it have been?

Mom looped a finger through the handle of her tea. "Do you remember the time, when you were about two and a half, that you fell asleep on your dad's lap and his snoring woke you up? You glared at him like you couldn't believe such a weird sound could come from inside him. Then you patted his cheek and told him to stop it."

I didn't remember, but the idea of it made me laugh until my eyes ran. "For real?"

"Oh yeah." Mom laughed too, and after that my family did regular things like it was any other day. My grandparents tended their garden, like normal. Mom made me eggs and toast, like normal. I showered, like normal, and texted Ciara and then went over to her house, like normal. For a little while it seemed as if everything would be normal from then on. Like Deirdre Redmond and the noise were just blips in an otherwise average July.

But by now you already know that wasn't what happened.

TWO

THE FIRST TIME I met Ciara, who lived six doors down from my grandparents' house, it was because her mom had run into my grandmother around the neighborhood. This was back when I was nine turning ten — the year we started spending Julys in Dublin. Gran suggested Mrs. Kavanagh bring Ciara over for my birthday barbecue because she was only a few months older than me. But at the party we didn't know what to say to each other until my dad came out of the house with toilet paper stuck to the bottom of his shoe, and then Ciara and I couldn't stop giggling. Each year since then I'd spent part of my vacation hanging out with her.

As I knocked on Ciara's front door, I was half-wondering if she still had a crush on her horseback riding instructor, Ryan. Last summer she'd talked about him so much that it was hard to get a word in edgewise, but Ciara and I rarely chatted or texted each other in between visits. It was like our friendship made more sense in person.

Mr. Kavanagh opened the door and ushered me inside the house, Ciara's darker-than-midnight German Shepherd–Labrador cross, Ripley, bounding over to me. She wagged her tail feverishly and nudged my fingers. I ran my right hand along the top of Ripley's head and she instantly dropped to the floor, rolling over to expose her belly. It was always funny to see a dog that could easily be mistaken for a black wolf act like a teddy bear, and I broke into a smile that Ciara interrupted when she clomped downstairs to tug me away.

We hurried up to her room and sat in the same spot beside her bed where we always sat, Ciara declaring, "You look exactly the same only taller."

Almost five foot six, giving me about four inches on Ciara. I couldn't say she looked the same as last year because Ciara had developed a whole new body since I'd last seen her. Between that and her makeup (lilac lip gloss, coral blush, and heavy eye mascara and eyeliner) she could easily have passed for fifteen.

"Are you still playing hockey?" she asked.

"Always." I flashed a grin. "Goalies rule." I wasn't under any illusion about being the next Hayley Wickenheiser, who had played pro for a guy's team in Finland and been on the Canadian women's Olympic team four times, but I loved hockey with a vengeance.

I was about to ask Ciara if she still had the Ouija board we'd been addicted to a couple of years back when she said, "I'm taking modeling classes as soon as I turn fourteen. Not that I want to be a model, but I'll need to know proper posture and stuff like that for what I really want to do."

"What's that?" I still had a whole year left before high school; I had no idea what I wanted to be yet.

"Entertainment journalism. You know, interviewing celebrities on telly."

I wrinkled my nose. "Wouldn't you rather be a real

journalist? Then you could be stationed in some cool place like Istanbul or Shanghai." Ciara was pretty different from my Kingston best friends — Alexis, Lily, and Taneisha — who all played hockey, just like me, and who weren't much into traditional girl things. But we used to be able to get through Julys on two similarities: an interest in paranormal stuff like ghosts and ESP and the way something funny could send us into a laughing jag we didn't know how to stop. Now that we felt even more different than usual, would those two things be enough?

Ciara arched her eyebrows. "That sounds too much like serious work." She tossed her head back, a sly grin stretching across her face. "Just wait'll you see Shehan. He's the opposite of you — he looks sooooo different from last summer."

"Different how?" Because the two of us and Shehan Ranaweera were pretty much the only kids on my grandparents' street, Ciara and I would hang out with Shehan sometimes, just talking or doing things like kicking around a soccer ball in one of our yards (mostly Shehan and me because Ciara got bored with sports fast).

But in all my Julys in Ireland I'd never heard Ciara sound excited about Shehan like she did when she lunged for her cellphone in her room that day. "He's dyed his hair deep blue and it's sort of shaved at the sides but spiky on top," she said. "I'll show you." Six seconds later Ciara shoved a digital picture of Shehan in my face. "Now, tell me he didn't get cute."

Shehan wasn't ever un-cute, but, like Ciara, he looked older, more mature than when I'd seen him last. Actually, he was a year older than us, fourteen since May. Staring at his image made me feel weird, like I was the only one of the three of us who was still the same old me.

"He's taller too," Ciara continued. "Taller than you." She tilted her head to one side as I took her phone and pretended not to be surprised by the distinctly teenage-looking Shehan.

"He changed his hair, but he still looks like Shehan," I told her. Before, his hair was always plain black and cut short. At home he would've been hard to find in a crowd. He only stood out in Ireland because his dad was British Sri Lankan, making him less pale than most people.

"Like new and improved Shehan," Ciara said knowingly. "We should go round and see him later so you can say hi."

I didn't try to talk Ciara out of the idea, but I was glad when it turned out Shehan wasn't home and we were left standing on his doorstep later. "I should've texted him," Ciara said. "But he can be woeful about checking his mobile sometimes."

That's what they called cellphones in Ireland, *mobiles*. How long had Ciara and Shehan had each other's numbers? They never used to text each other.

"We'll catch him next time," I said, and when I got back to my grandparents' house I realized that not only had I forgotten to tell Ciara about Deirdre Redmond swinging a frying pan at my granddad, it had completely slipped my mind to ask whether she still had a thing for Ryan.

DAY THREE

The next morning my grandparents, mom, and I drove up to my aunt Fiona's house, well outside of Dublin. My cousin Megan was doing theater set design in Edinburgh, so it was just Aunt Fiona and Uncle Brendan left at the house in Cavan they operated as a B&B. The place had a huge backyard where we all played croquet and then sat around eating tuna wraps and couscous salad while staring into the sun and listening to Uncle Brendan play guitar.

It was never anywhere near as hot in Dublin as it got in Kingston, and Irish people were constantly joking about the bad weather. But on that particular day everyone was just relishing the heat, so when I got thirsty and Aunt Fiona said she'd go into the kitchen to get me another drink I didn't want her to have to leave the sunshine. I told her I'd grab it myself and went in through the back door, striding past the laundry room and into the kitchen, where Gran was standing in the middle of the tile floor. She looked like someone who'd just heard bad news and didn't know what to do about it.

Gran cleared her throat when she saw me, the tension draining from her face. "For the life of me I can't remember why I came into the kitchen." She laughed lightly, one of her hands flying to her hair to push it back behind her ears. "I thought I'd wait around a minute and see if it came back to me."

"Maybe you wanted a drink," I suggested. "It's pretty warm outside."

Gran tilted her head and mulled over my suggestion. "I don't think that's it." Her eyes swept over the countertop and cupboards before returning to mine. "You know, I can't remember what I'm doing here. Isn't that strange?" She took a step closer to the nearest cupboard and pulled it open. Her fingers absently brushed against a ceramic bowl. "Is this your kitchen?"

"No, Gran, it's Fiona and Brendan's. We came to visit them in Cavan." Mom had warned me Gran's memory would get worse, but she'd made it sound like it would take more time.

"Of course, yes." Gran gently closed the cupboard. "I'm being silly. Of course, it's Fiona and Brendan's house. They've lived here for years."

Gran never did recall what had brought her into the kitchen in the first place, but the two of us glanced at each other from across the room when Granddad couldn't find his car keys later that night. Everyone joined in the search, and eventually Aunt Fiona stumbled across his keychain on the entertainment unit in the living room.

"Funny," Granddad said gruffly, "I can't remember putting them there in the first place."

"Must be the key fairies having a laugh at your expense," Aunt Fiona teased.

The group of us traded goodbye hugs, and Aunt Fiona and Uncle Brendan said they'd see me the following weekend for my birthday barbecue. I already knew Ciara and Shehan would be there too. Gran invited them and their parents every year, and she'd told me that Ciara's mom and Shehan's dad had been in touch to say they were coming.

On the drive back to Dublin, both Granddad and Gran broke out in dry coughs. Gran was constantly armed with a package of mints and pressed one into my granddad's hand.

"You two are coming down with something," Mom observed when Granddad choked up for the fourth or fifth time.

"It's just a tickle," Granddad countered. "Nothing a cup of tea won't fix."

"Actually, I do feel a bit off," Gran admitted, fiddling with her hair like she had in Aunt Fiona's kitchen. "A bit achy, and a bit foggy in the head as well. I think I'll get into bed when we get home."

About twenty minutes later we were turning off Haverhill Road (the main road stretching the length of Haverhill, the Southside area of Dublin where my grandparents resided) and onto Birchwood Street. Sykes Close, where Gran and Granddad lived, was just off Birchwood. We were nearly home. It was almost nine-thirty but still light out when I suddenly got the second flash of Shehan Ranaweera that I'd had this year.

I squinted at his image through the rear window. He was cruising along the sidewalk on the same red mountain bike I remembered from last year, wearing dark jeans and a checkered hoodie, a knapsack on his back. I couldn't specifically tell that he was taller, but his shoulders looked wider and he was less wiry in general. If Ciara hadn't shown me his photo, the spiky blue haircut would've thrown me so much that I probably wouldn't have recognized him.

But I did, and I cried, "Hey, there's Shehan. Can you pull over, Granddad?"

My grandfather began steering the car to the curb as Mom objected, "Naomi, it's late. You can see him tomorrow."

"Come on, Mom. Just for a couple minutes. I haven't seen him in a whole year."

My mother relented. "Only a couple minutes."

I swung the door open, calling out Shehan's name.

He looked over his shoulder and turned on the sidewalk. "Hiya," he called, smiling brightly as he pedaled towards me. "When'd you get here?"

I smiled back. "Friday night. I saw Ciara already."

"She told me you two came round while I was out." One of Shehan's feet landed on the ground for balance, the other rested on a bike pedal. His knapsack was open at the top, something that looked like a flute case jutting out of it.

Shehan's vivid hazel eyes looked the same as ever — it was just the rest of his face that had grown up a little — and I forgot to think of him as a teenage guy and impulsively reached out to tap the black case in his knapsack, like he was the same boy I'd known for years. "What's this? Are you playing the flute now or something?"

Shehan laughed. The sound was definitely deeper than the laugh that used to spill from his throat. "*The flute*," he repeated. "Do I look like a flute player? No, it's a snooker cue. I've been playing at the local club. It keeps me out of trouble."

Once he'd said it I remembered that he'd been playing snooker a bit the summer before too. I knew he was kidding about the keeping him out of trouble part because I also remembered Shehan wanted to be a cop — or a guard, as they called them in Ireland. "So, is that where you're coming from?"

"Yeah, it's not far. I usually cycle over. What about you?" He cocked his head at the now empty roadway. "Out with your gran and granddad?"

I told him about our visit to Aunt Fiona and then the squealing noise and Deirdre Redmond incident from the day before.

"Are you serious?" Shehan said, stunned. "I've never seen her act like that. She always says hello to me by name."

"My mom said the same — that she didn't have any memory problems or anything." Suddenly I felt bad for gossiping. If Mrs. Redmond was sick in some way it wasn't her fault, just like it wasn't Gran's fault. "Anyway, I better get home. I just wanted to say hi."

"Hi," Shehan repeated, his long eyelashes blinking slowly like he wasn't done looking at me. It made me feel sort of shy but also like I was having a sugar rush, which was stupid because he was just Shehan with new hair. Shehan, I reminded myself. This is your friend Shehan. *You've heard his dad yell at him for not taking out the trash and you've burped in front of each other when you've gulped down Coca-Cola too fast. You've kicked a ball around his backyard together, the two of you blindfolded because everything normal was boring you that day, and you didn't stop playing until you'd collided hard twice and then broken a flowerpot.*

The very first time I'd met Shehan, three summers earlier, Ciara and I had been walking Ripley while her dad watched over us from their front stoop. Ripley started to trek through a big brown puddle in the middle of the sidewalk and Ciara tugged her to the left, onto the lawn, to avoid it. Neither of us heard the bicycle charging up behind us, and the boy, who had already been swerving to pass us, didn't have enough room to clear both Ciara on his right side and the tree on his left. He crashed straight into the tree trunk and ended up in a heap on the grass along with his bike.

Ciara, her dad, and I leapt over to the boy to make sure he was okay. Shehan insisted he was fine with such stubbornness that Mr. Kavanagh gave in and left the three of us standing there, Ciara asking Shehan a slew of nosy questions he ignored. The only thing he'd really wanted to talk about was a slasher movie he'd seen a few days earlier, and when we finally walked away Ciara whispered, "What a weirdo."

Later we found out Shehan's mom had died a few months earlier. That was probably what had made him so quiet in the beginning, and while Ciara didn't entirely stop thinking Shehan was weird, she got used to him.

But I'd always been the one who got along better with Shehan. Until this summer.

Now my mind leapt over all the Julys Shehan and I had known each other, making an off-balance landing back in the present.

"You're coming to the barbecue next weekend, right?" I said, half-swiveling to leave.

"Your birthday barbecue," Shehan noted. "I'll be there. What age will you be then? Thirteen?"

"Yep. The big one-three." Before we left Kingston, my dad had teased that he wasn't ready for me to turn into a teenager yet because next thing he knew I'd be acting moody with everyone, sleeping until noon, playing bad music so loudly that the neighbors complained, and bringing home a boyfriend he didn't like.

"Ancient," Shehan said, stretching out the word in a way that made me grin.

"Almost as ancient as you."

"Ah, you'll never catch up." The way Shehan's eyes sparkled made my face warm. "You know what they say; you should respect your elders."

"No chance of that if we're talking about me respecting you," I joked, resisting the urge to thump his shoulder like I would've in the past. *Could we still do that with each other now?*

Shehan was still looking at me, but it had turned into more of a regular look. "I'll walk with you," he said. He climbed off his bike and we strode in the direction of my grandparents' house, Shehan telling me that his sister, Sara, was staying in England for all but two weeks of the summer. She'd just finished her first year at University College London and was taking courses during the summer session too. "The swot," he declared.

"My dad's not going to be around for most of the summer either," I said. "He's back home looking after the café he bought with my aunt."

Shehan pointed out Deirdre Redmond's house, and we both got quiet as we neared it. The lights were off, the drapes closed tight, and the driveway empty.

Soon we were standing in front of my gran and granddad's place. Shehan said, "You should give me your mobile number so we can text." I offered him my digits, and he texted me right away so I'd have his number too.

"It's good to see you again," he said as we tucked our phones away. "You're looking well."

"Tall," I joked, feeling funny again under his gaze.

"That too. But it's not what I meant." Shehan's eyes were sheepish, and suddenly I felt mine get sheepish too. Like I wouldn't know how to act if Shehan was going to be a teenage guy and me a teenage girl.

We said goodbye, and I'd only just walked through the front door when my cell beeped. I was expecting it to be Shehan again, or maybe my dad texting to say goodnight like he usually did, but instead it was Ciara wanting to know if I'd come to the Fun Fair in Bray with her tomorrow. I zipped through the hallway and into the living room, searching for my mom to let her know I was back and to ask about the fair.

Granddad was alone in the room, drinking the cup of tea he'd said would set him right while watching the news from his favorite armchair. "Hello, love," he murmured. "How's the boy, then?"

I barely heard what the newscaster was saying in the background, something about a virus that had been affecting senior citizens. Typical. They hardly ever told happy stories on the news. I tuned out the TV and replied, "Shehan's good. Playing lots of pool. I mean, snooker. Do you know where Mom is, Granddad?"

"In the cistin," he mumbled.

"The *cistin*?" My eyebrows knit together in confusion.

"The kitchen," he repeated, suddenly grumpy. "The

kitchen, I said."

That wasn't what he'd said, but I didn't correct my grandfather. People with colds — because that's all I thought it was — were allowed to be a little cranky.

THREE

DAY FOUR

THE NEXT DAY Mr. Kavanagh drove us out to Bray for the Fun Fair in his minivan. Ciara's nine-year-old half-brother, Adam, and a friend of his, a kid with red hair and freckle splotches, made underarm noises in the back seat until Ciara yelled at Adam to stop. Mr. and Mrs. Kavanagh had been separated for a while years ago, and that's when Adam happened. Ciara didn't tell me about him until we were eleven, and she usually frowned when she mentioned him. "He's going to do my head in," she complained as we hopped onto the Sizzler together at the fair. "And he'll be with us all summer because his mother is off doing community development work in Kilimanjaro."

But Ciara perked up a little more with each ride we boarded. We screamed, laughed, and howled as we were catapulted into the sky, spun relentlessly in circles, and jerked mercilessly from side to side. On the Crazy Mouse, as we were cruising up a hill in a painted red mouse cart while sitting next to two girls speaking Mandarin, I remembered to ask Ciara about Ryan.

"He's still irresistible, but he's too old for me," she admitted. "He's, like, twenty, and I think he's going out with one of the other horseback riding instructors."

The wind caught my hair as we hurled down the coaster hill, the two of us squealing. At the bottom, Ciara picked up where the conversation had left off and wanted to know if I liked anyone. "I bet you meet a lot of fit boy hockey players," she added.

"Not really." By *fit* she meant cute, but I played hockey with other girls and only saw most of the boy players in passing, and most of the guys I knew from school were just friends. Meanwhile, Shehan popped into my head for no good reason at all.

Mr. Kavanagh was waiting for us when we got off the Crazy Mouse, and after Adam and his friend scooted over too, we all devoured sloppy pizza slices and then played carnival games. Adam won a stuffed shark, which Mr. Kavanagh offered to carry after Adam dropped it and a lady nearly tripped over its fin. While we strolled around the fairground, it was hard not to notice the teenage boys eyeing up Ciara. I saw her smile back a couple of times, and if Mr. Kavanagh hadn't been with us one or two of the boys might've tried to talk to her.

Once we'd done everything there was to do and were finally bored with the fair, Mr. Kavanagh bought five ice cream cones and we walked the Bray promenade. "You're not interested in guys yet, are you?" Ciara said knowingly. "You're still *twelve* twelve, even though you're about to turn thirteen."

"*Twelve* twelve?" I echoed sarcastically. I knew what she meant: I was immature. A kid. And maybe she was right, because I couldn't help launching into an imitation of the last guy who'd been ogling Ciara, fluttering my eyelashes, squaring my jaw, and looking her up and down. "You have to admit it was kind of funny the way he was staring at you, as though you were going to find his squinting eyes irresistible and chase after him." I lengthened my stride and swung my arms, my swagger matching the boy's. "Whoah. Look how cool I am."

Ciara hiccupped out a laugh and knocked her shoulder against mine. "*Twelve* twelve," she taunted, but she was laughing harder as she said it. I was still doing my random-boy-in-lust-with-Ciara impression, but I started to laugh too. And next thing I knew we were both losing our breath, bent over and full-out giggling like we were *five* five.

After that I didn't worry whether the two things we had in common would be enough to last the summer. Everything felt just like always.

On our way back to Haverhill, the sky began to darken and fat drops dotted the minivan's windows. Mr. Kavanagh drove Adam's friend home first and then let me off at the end of my grandparents' driveway. I thought I heard distant thunder as I raced for the door.

"I'm back!" I shouted as I charged inside. There was no reply from within, just the sound of the TV up loud.

I kicked off my shoes and ambled into the living room, where Gran was sitting in Granddad's favorite chair. Her hands were folded firmly together in her lap and she was glued to the television. I didn't think I'd ever seen her so fixated on *anything*, and my eyes dashed to the screen like there must have been something monumentally important

on the screen. News of a world war breaking out, or a cure
for cancer.

Instead it was one of those home decorating shows
where designers make your house look brand new inside
overnight. Gran glanced at me from the corner of her eyes
but stayed quiet. Normally she'd have showered me with
questions about my day, but her silence and the way she
refused to face me were so unnerving that I didn't say anything either. Instead I continued to the kitchen, goosebumps
erupting on my skin.

Granddad and Mom were locked in a mute stare when
I bounded into the room, each of them leaning against opposite counters. Granddad's angry slash of a mouth twitched,
and Mom's face was pointed with anxiety. "Naomi, please
go up to your room," Mom commanded. "I'll be up in a
minute."

"What's happening?"

Mom shook her head wearily. "I'll be up in a minute,"
she repeated.

My heart was galloping as I backed out of the room,
Granddad lashing out the moment I was gone. "You tell me
where your brothers and sister are this second," he roared.
"They were told not to leave the house." His words were
punctuated by a thump, which I visualized as his hand
smacking the counter.

"I'm going to get Fiona on the phone for you right now,
Dad," Mom insisted. "But if you'll just sit down and have
a think about Mark and Declan I'm sure you'll remember
they're in Australia." Firm as her tone was, it didn't entirely
cover the fear in Mom's voice.

On the other side of the living room door I didn't stop to look at Gran by the TV, I just rocketed into the hall, the sound of my mother's voice fading. How could my granddad forget that my uncles had moved to Australia when they'd been gone for twenty years? Gran was the one with memory problems — the one we needed to be patient with. Only now there was Deirdre Redmond, Gran, and Granddad all changing so quickly I couldn't keep up.

Up in my room I sat on the floor with my back against the wardrobe, listening for noises from downstairs. Soon I heard low voices on the stairs. A door shutting. Something creaking, A box spring maybe. The rasp of a cough seeping through my wall.

Over half an hour passed before there was a rap at my door and Mom swung it open. Her spine and jaw were stiff as she crossed towards me at the foot of the wardrobe. "I convinced your granddad to go back to bed," she said in a near-whisper. "He was up here almost all day, not feeling well. When he came down he seemed pretty agitated and then —"

"How come he can't remember about Uncle Mark and Uncle Declan," I interrupted. "And Gran, she was just sitting there staring at the TV, not saying anything."

Mom folded her arms tightly in front of her. "To tell you the truth, I don't have any explanation for what's going on. She's been quiet like that most of the day, only saying a word or two at a time and he ... well, just before he went up he seemed to remember about Mark and Declan again. I could literally see it all come back to him." Mom drew her right hand across her worried brow. "I wanted to take them both to hospital, but when I suggested it your granddad only got more agitated. I'm hoping he'll be more reasonable after a good night's sleep."

I didn't say anything about Deirdre Redmond. I didn't need to; I knew we were both thinking about her. "Have you told Dad?" I asked.

Mom shook her head, tugging at the belt on her cardigan. "I want to call the Redmond house first and find out how Mrs. Redmond is doing, and then get in touch with Mr. or Mrs. Kavanagh to see if they'd mind having you over tomorrow while I'm at the hospital." Mom must have been expecting me to protest because she added, "I know you're fine on your own, but I don't want to leave you alone here while this is going on."

I didn't object the way I usually would've. Better to be at Ciara's than sitting home by myself worrying about Gran and Granddad.

Mom went to make her phone calls and then came back to confirm that it was all right for me to go over to Ciara's house the next day. Unfortunately, Mom's call to Deirdre Redmond's house had gone unanswered. Later still, when I was lying in bed wondering whether Mom had been able to pry Gran away from the TV or if she'd still be sitting there tomorrow morning, my cellphone rang.

"Are you holding up okay there, Naomi?" Dad said, popping onto my screen.

Mom must have called him already, and it was good to see his face, but I wished he weren't so far away. "I'm all right. I just hope they can help Gran and Granddad at the hospital."

"They will," Dad said. "You know your granddad has never had any problems with his memory before, and the sudden changes with Gran are unusual too. The doctors will figure out whatever's going on and nurse them back to health." Dad changed the subject, staying on the phone with me for fifteen minutes and making me give him details about the Fun Fair before describing his busy day at the café.

The conversation didn't really distract me like I'm sure he wanted it to, but after we hung up I did feel a little better than before he'd called. Better enough to sleep.

DAY FIVE

When I woke up that morning, golden sunlight was streaming through my window with such force that I almost believed the day before had been a bad dream. Outside I heard birds chirping and a lone dog bark. The sounds were comfortingly normal, and I burrowed under the covers for an extra minute before convincing myself to move.

I'd only begun to sit up in bed when my door opened. Granddad peeked inside at me and gave his head a shake, like I should already be out of bed. "You'll be late for school, Noleen," he admonished. "Hurry, now."

Noleen was my mother's name. I'd seen pictures of her when she was fourteen (wearing roller skates and a satin jacket and standing with her arms draped around her friends' shoulders) and I did look a lot like she had back then. I wasn't sure whether I should correct my grandfather or not. I sat there trying to make my mind up for so long that Granddad closed the door.

The sun was nearly blinding as I stumbled out of bed and pulled on my clothes, bracing myself for whatever would happen next. Downstairs I found Mom, Granddad, and Gran gathered around the kitchen table, eating porridge. "Hi, Naomi," Mom said, flashing me a warning look.

Granddad gazed up at me, his chin dipping. "I'm sorry about what I said up there, pet. I don't know what's wrong with me. I can't seem to hold on to the moment. Your mother's going to take us to hospital when we finish here."

"They'll figure it out, Granddad," I told him, echoing what my dad had said on the phone the night before.

"Course they will." My grandfather reached out to cover Gran's hand with his own. Gran herself said nothing. She continued to spoon porridge into her mouth, pausing only to cough briefly.

I fished a bowl out of one of the cupboards behind my head and then grabbed the Rice Krispies and milk. Nobody said much while we ate. I was the last one finished. We left the dirty dishes piled in the sink, and Mom led my grandparents out to Granddad's car, me trailing behind them. Granddad hesitated before climbing into the back seat. "Where are we going?" he asked. "I think I'd rather stay in today."

He'd lost hold of the present again, and Mom smiled thinly. "Just out for a short drive in the country, Dad. It'll be fun."

She bundled Gran into the passenger seat and then hugged me fast. "I'll call you when I have news."

I stood in the driveway waving goodbye to the three

of them. Nearby a dog barked again. It could have been Ripley, and I walked quickly to Ciara's house, in a hurry not to be alone.

It was Mr. Kavanagh who was home with Ciara and Adam again and who let me in. Ciara wasn't awake yet, so I sat in the living room watching a kids' TV show with Adam until she came downstairs and asked, "What's wrong with your gran and granddad?"

"We don't know yet," I said curtly. And I didn't want to talk about it.

Ciara pursed her lips and skimmed my arm. "They'll be okay."

I watched Ciara eat yogurt and a banana for breakfast. Afterwards she showered and insisted on buffing and painting our nails. I think she was trying to make me feel better, but it took her so long to finish that it was nearly lunchtime. Her dad made us cheese and pickle sandwiches, and once we'd eaten we went for a long walk with Ripley, past the Spar (sort of like a 7-Eleven) on Haverhill Road and down a side street where an Anglican church sprawled.

We ended up at a park, where Ciara plopped herself down on the grass and angled her face up to the sun, Ripley sitting obediently next to her. "My dad won't care if we're gone for a while," she said. "Adam keeps him busy enough. He's a pain in the neck. You're lucky you're an only child."

My fingers brushed through the overgrown park grass as I dropped down on the other side of Ciara. I spied a beetle attached to one of the shorter blades near my thumb and pointed it out to her.

"Gross," she said. "They're so ugly."

"*Spiders* are ugly," I countered. "The creepy way they move." I hated that I was a wimp when it came to spiders. It was ridiculous to be afraid of something a fraction of your size, unless it happened to be poisonous or carrying an infectious disease. "But this beetle's sort of pretty. Look at its shell." The bug's green metallic casing glimmered in the sun.

Ciara gazed more closely at the beetle's sheen, like she was trying to see my point. "Spiders are worse. But I wouldn't exactly call this pretty."

Meanwhile, Ripley yawned like we were boring her to pieces. Sometimes I would've sworn that she understood English. My friend Alexis back home had a dog, but you could tell it wasn't smart like Ripley, and it stuck to her mom like a third arm or leg, as though everyone else in the universe was potentially a serial killer.

Then suddenly Ripley was on her feet, barking like a genuine guard dog. My eyes zoomed in the direction she was facing. A dark blue sedan was driving straight for us, moving at a crawl — slow enough to jog alongside — but still, no one but park maintenance staff should've been driving through a park. Ciara and I jumped to our feet and dashed out of the way. The car continued cruising in a straight line, heading for a collection of holly bushes.

I got a glimpse of white collar inside a black shirt as the sedan neared. A gray-haired priest rolled down the window, waving frantically at us. "I don't know how to stop it," he shouted. "Help me!"

The brakes must not have been working, and he was running out of park. Soon he'd be back on the road, where he was bound to crash into something, no matter how slowly the car was moving.

I sprinted after the car, acting on instinct. "Grab the emergency brake," I yelled, running in line with the driver's seat so he'd hear me. The priest's jaw dropped, his eyes radiating panic. He didn't understand what I was telling him.

"The lever next to you. Pull it!" I made the motion with my hand, reaching out for air, closing my fist around it, and yanking it towards me.

The sedan jolted to a stop in the middle of the holly bushes, anxious voices behind me. I spun to find Ciara and Ripley in my wake. Two women my mom's age were about fifteen yards away from us, dashing across the park in shoes that weren't meant for running. One of them was shouting, "Father Mahoney! Father Mahoney!" while the other called, "Stop, Father!" and then, "Girls, girls, thank God, he didn't hit you." It would've seemed almost comical if the air hadn't been tinged with fear.

Because Ciara and I were closer to the priest than the women were, I kept going until I reached the car. Planting my hands on the door, I lowered my head to the driver's window and cried, "Are you okay?"

The priest pressed his eyelids slowly together. He inclined his head a single time as he opened his eyes. "I couldn't think how to stop it," he murmured. "Just couldn't remember."

Without warning, the man who must have been Father Mahoney jerked to open the door. I hopped back. "I'm sorry," he said, climbing out of the car. His panic had sharpened into a terror that made his hands quake. "I don't think this is the right place for me — the car. It will ..." He took a sweeping look around the park and then down at the trampled holly bushes. "It will have to be towed."

"Don't worry about that now," one of the middle-aged women told him. They'd caught up with us, the thinner lady huffing and puffing and the other standing tall but visibly shaken. "Everybody's in one piece. That's the main thing."

The thinner lady edged past Ciara, Ripley, and me to dive into the car and retrieve the keys from the ignition. It stopped humming, lifeless as a stone.

"Let's go," I said, touching Ciara's sleeve. "They can take care of this." Goosebumps formed on my skin just like they had the night before at the sight of my grandmother acting catatonic. This forgetting had happened too many times for it to be any kind of coincidence.

"*But*," Ciara began to say. Then she saw the look on my face and stood closer to me. "Okay." Ripley dropped her head and began to growl as we moved away from the trio. She kept stopping in her tracks to look at them, and I couldn't help thinking it was the priest in particular she was growling at. If you knew Ripley, you'd know she didn't just growl for no reason. I'd only seen her growl twice — one time at a guy in his twenties who was staring at me and Ciara funny and the other at a house on Haverhill Road that Ciara said she *always* growled at. I guessed maybe Ripley sensed something about the house that people couldn't. Something like I was sensing in the park — the feeling that something was really the matter.

Whatever it was, my instincts told me to get as far away from it as possible, and I strode away as swiftly as

my legs would carry me, forcing Ciara to pick up the pace
and Ripley to turn away from the priest and the women
helping him.

FOUR

ON THE WAY back to Ciara's house I told her about my grandparents and Deirdre Redmond, and she was instantly as spooked as I was. When we repeated everything for Mr. Kavanagh, though, he peered doubtfully out from black-rimmed glasses. "Look, it must have given you girls a fright seeing that car drive through the middle of the park, but trust me," he said, "there's nothing out of the ordinary going on. Many people have problems with their memories when they get older, and there are a lot of senior citizens in this area. It's not something to be afraid of. They're just people who need our help and understanding."

Sykes Close definitely had lots of older people living on it. When I wasn't there, Shehan and Ciara were the only two people our age on the road. I'd seen a woman with a stroller a few times, and I guessed there might be some parents with little kids or babies, but practically everyone else was over sixty. But that wasn't the point.

"I'm *not* afraid of people with memory problems," I said stubbornly. "If you saw what happened like we did you wouldn't think it was Alzheimer's or some other kind of dementia." Whatever was happening was affecting too many people, too quickly. As though it were catching. "This is more like mass amnesia hitting people out of the blue."

Surprise gusted across Mr. Kavanagh's face; he'd expected me to agree with him. "What did you say the priest's name was?" he asked, switching his attention to Ciara. "I'm going to ring the guards and find out whether he has a license that needs to be revoked. I hate to do it, but having someone driving around in that condition is extremely dangerous."

"Father Mahoney," Ciara replied.

Mr. Kavanagh left the room to make the call, and Adam, who must've overheard at least some of the things we'd said, drifted into the kitchen and stared at us sideways. "What?" Ciara snapped, now doubly agitated because of her half-brother's presence.

"Did you really almost get run over by a crazy priest?" he asked, jutting out his chin.

"He wasn't crazy," I answered. I hated to think of anyone calling my gran crazy just because she couldn't remember things. It wasn't right.

Adam folded his arms in front of him and held his elbows. "Not remembering how to use brakes is crazy. I've never even driven a car and I'd know how to use the brakes."

"You'd have crashed the car worse than he did," Ciara said. "You'd probably have run everyone down because your feet wouldn't reach the pedals."

"If my feet wouldn't reach the pedals I wouldn't be able to hit the gas either, so how would I run anyone over?" Adam asked, wiggling his eyebrows and smirking a little.

Ciara sighed heavily, like Adam had given her a lot of

practise at it. "Was anyone talking to you in the first place? Mind your own business."

Adam skulked away, and Ciara and I went up to her room where she turned her iPod on loudly, flopped onto her bed with her phone, and texted Shehan to tell him what had happened at the park. Eventually Mrs. Kavanagh arrived home and we had a chicken casserole for dinner. I pushed the food around my plate, only finishing half of it because I couldn't stop thinking about how long Mom had been gone with Gran and Granddad.

After dinner I tried to call Mom's cell, but there was no answer. Then Ciara got a text from Shehan and texted him back, asking him to come over. Soon the three of us were sitting on the patio furniture in Ciara's backyard with Ripley hanging out at the center of our circle. The sky had turned a medium gray that could've meant rain, but then again, maybe not. It wasn't cold or warm, just blah. If it was going to rain I wished it would just make up its mind to do it and start already.

Shehan stretched his legs out in front of him, his hazel eyes landing on me. "Have you heard any updates about your gran and granddad?"

I didn't have to worry about Ciara picking up on any new feelings I was having for Shehan; I was too distracted to feel anything except anxious about my grandparents. "Nothing yet." I reached down to pet Ripley. She was sort of like a stress ball — touching her felt therapeutic.

"You reckon the priest in the park had the same thing as them and Mrs. Redmond?" he asked. "Like something in the water causing it?"

"My gran has Alzheimer's disease — she was repeating herself and things like that before. Forgetting things."

"I didn't know that." Shehan sat taller in his chair.

"My mom said it was in the early stages. But I mean, she wouldn't even talk today. It seemed really different." I frowned into my hand. "If it was something in the water we'd all have it, wouldn't we?"

"Maybe." Shehan leaned forward. "There was an old fella at the club earlier today who forgot where he was right in the middle of a match. One of his neighbors had to take him home. I only know him to see, so he could have memory problems all the time, but with what you two have said, I don't know …"

Ciara tapped one of Shehan's running shoes with hers. "You never said anything about him in your text."

"I thought it'd keep for a few minutes until I got here." The hint of a smile flitted across his lips. "You just hate to wait for anything, don't you?"

Ciara's eyes brightened as she stared back at him. I stealth-glanced at the two of them, feeling as if I'd missed the beginning of the conversation, although I'd been there the entire time.

Ciara rearranged her face into a mini-scowl, pretending to be annoyed at Shehan's remark. "I think you're confusing me with *you*," she said, a vibe running between Ciara and Shehan that you'd have to be blind and deaf not to pick up on. His expression, when he looked at her, was just like those guys at the Fun Fair.

The thought stung, but I had more important things to worry about.

Shehan's attention stayed with Ciara for two seconds before switching back to me. "Maybe it's a side effect of some medication they're all on," he theorized, scratching at his ear. "A bad batch of cholesterol pills or something. Every old person I know is on medication for something. Do you know what kind of pills your grandparents take?"

"Gran's on something for her thyroid." I'd seen her take it with a gulp of water lots of times over the years. "And a pill for her memory that she takes at night. My grand-dad's on medication too." Light brown caplets. "But I don't know what it is."

My phone rang in my pocket. I fished it out, conscious of my friends' gazes on me as I listened to Mom say she was on her way home and would pick me up at Ciara's in about fifteen minutes.

"What about Gran and Granddad?" I asked, staring down at Ripley.

"They're staying at the hospital," Mom said tiredly. "I'll fill you in when I get there."

"Okay." My voice was itchy, and when Mom and I hung up Shehan looked away from me. "She's coming to pick me up soon," I announced.

Neither of them asked about my grandparents. They must have guessed it was bad news. Shehan's eyes scoured the yard. "Where's Ripley's ball?" he asked. "I'll throw her a few before I leave."

Ciara pointed. "Down by the shed." The Kavanaghs had one of those fetch toys that grip the ball so you didn't have to reach down and pick it up when it was coated in dog-mouth goo. I saw the toy lying near a garden bed by the shed too. "But you're going already?" she added.

Shehan was loping across the lawn. He turned to answer her. "Yeah, I should head, especially with Naomi's mum and everything." Shehan's gaze floated to me. If I hadn't just seen him and Ciara flirting I might've thought there was an extra helping of concern in his eyes.

The three of us took turns throwing the ball for Ripley and then trying to wrestle it from her jaws. She was having the time of her life; she could probably have done that all night so long as someone would've brought her water every once in a while. But then Shehan went home and Mrs. Kavanagh came out to say my mom had arrived. She was smiling when she said it, and I wished it were the kind of smile I could believe in, but I knew the kind of smile someone gives you when they're trying to pretend everything's okay and Mrs. Kavanagh's was a textbook example.

"Text me later," Ciara said.

I nodded numbly and followed my mom out to the car, the sky darker and more threatening with every step.

FIVE

ACCORDING TO MY mom there was a crowd of senior citizens at the hospital with the same symptoms as my grandparents. The doctor and nurses said it was some kind of virus that was hitting the elderly population hard. Other than that, Mom didn't tell me much, only that she didn't know when Gran and Granddad would be home, but that the doctors were taking good care of them. She went upstairs to call my dad from the bedroom she usually shared with him when they were visiting my grandparents together.

The house felt empty with just Mom and me in it, and I texted Alexis in Kingston before remembering she was on vacation in California this week, probably doing cannonballs into a swimming pool at that very moment. I was in the middle of texting Lily when a message came in from Shehan, asking if I'd seen the news.

"What news?" I replied.

"Turn on your telly," he advised.

I flicked on the remote and motored through the channels until I reached Irish news. A reporter was speaking to a red-haired doctor in scrubs as he walked hurriedly away from a hospital building. "I'm not the one to comment on this," the doctor said reluctantly. "There's going to be a press conference at one o'clock tomorrow that will answer all your questions."

"In the meantime, what advice would you offer people having significant health problems?" the reporter asked doggedly. "Should they still seek treatment in their local hospitals?"

The red-headed doctor drew a short breath before answering her. "If they're in serious crisis, they should come into a hospital. Otherwise, they should see their doctor or wait it out at home until there's a public health update." He climbed abruptly into his car and drove off.

The broadcast cut back to the studio, where the newscaster summed up what they'd learned during the afternoon and evening. Hospitals across the nation had seen an increase in the admission of elderly patients beginning two to three days earlier. The spike in senior citizen admissions had multiplied exponentially today, and the media had discovered that many of those patients were suffering from sudden amnesia-like symptoms rather than a common flu.

Hearing about the sickness on the news made it sound much more serious than what my mom had said. My brain was spinning as a middle-aged couple was interviewed in the studio about their mother/mother-in-law's condition upon admittance to the hospital the previous afternoon. I couldn't just sit there and listen anymore; my fingers punched in Shehan's phone number.

His cell only rang once before he answered it. "Did you see it?" he asked.

The way my heart was thumping it was hard to get my

thoughts out. "Yeah, I saw. It sounds —"

"Unreal," Shehan finished. "How're your gran and granddad?"

I told him that my mom didn't know when they'd be released and explained about how they'd been acting over the last couple of days.

"*Cistin* means kitchen in Irish," Shehan said. "So it wasn't like your granddad made the word up out of nowhere."

Granddad must've learned Irish in his school days, like everyone in the country seemed to. I guessed his use of the word was Granddad jumping back to an earlier time in his head, same as when he'd thought I was my mother and couldn't remember about my uncles moving to Australia. With Deirdre Redmond it had been a poem. Maybe she'd learned it in school too.

"They both had a cough," I said. "Maybe that's part of the virus too. Maybe that's how it starts out." My feet were itching to move, and I leapt up and paced the room, Shehan running theories about the virus with me until I heard Mom's footsteps on the stairs.

She had Dad on the phone, and I said goodbye to Shehan and then listened to my father tell me that if my grandparents hadn't turned a corner within the next couple of days he was going to book an early flight to Dublin. He said that he could even be there by the weekend, and while I knew that wouldn't change my grandparents' condition, I felt happier just thinking about him being with Mom and me.

DAY SIX

I woke up early the next morning and began thinking
about my grandparents being sick all over again. When the
landline rang I gave up on the idea of going back to sleep
and headed downstairs. Mom was on the kitchen phone,
standing gray and frozen like a statue.

"I understand," she said into the phone in a brittle voice.
"We're in exactly the same boat."

I could only hear Mom's side of the conversation as I
opened the cupboard and sat down at the table to eat breakfast, but it didn't take a genius to figure out what she was
talking about.

Once she'd hung up, Mom sat down at the table with
me and wrapped her hands around the back of her neck.
"That was Deirdre Redmond's daughter. She saw me leaving the hospital yesterday and tried to catch up with me."
Mom smoothed one hand across the forest green placemat
in front of her. "The good news is that aside from a bit of
a cough, physically her mother's fine, but mentally ..."

Mom hesitated and I ventured, "Worse?"

Mom's hand was still skating back and forth across the
placemat. "We just have to stay positive and watch the
conference later. Maybe they'll have some good news."

Mom and I were both parked in front of the television by ten to one that afternoon. My cell was in my lap
because Ciara and I'd been texting. She was at home
waiting for the broadcast with her dad and brother, and
I bet Shehan was watching too. Mom planned to visit the
hospital afterwards but thought it would be better if I
didn't come with her.

I couldn't get comfortable on the couch. I kept adjusting my posture — pulling my feet up on the cushion with me and then planting them on the ground again. But when the news started I went absolutely still, my eyes stuck to the television. The same newscaster from last night was sitting in the studio. He said they were cutting live to the medical conference where a microbiologist from Trinity College and Ireland's Chief Medical Officer would speak. The microbiologist went first, explaining that patients over the age of sixty-five were flooding accident and emergency departments across Ireland.

"We are now referring to the previously unknown, highly infectious virus they're suffering with as amnestic-delirium syndrome," she continued. "An exposed person will begin to show symptoms of illness within one to five days. One of the symptoms is a low-grade fever. There's also a minor respiratory component which allows it to spread like the common cold, in this case mainly through cough secretions. But the more serious impact is on the infected person's memory. At first the memory disruption is temporary, but as the virus rapidly progresses, short- and then long-term memory is severely impaired."

The longer the microbiologist talked, the worse the news seemed. No one outside of the Republic had reported such an infection, but with the aggressive nature of the virus and lack of knowledge regarding its treatment, the World Health Organization would be issuing a travel advisory recommending limiting travel to Ireland. The Chief Medical Officer took over at the podium and announced, "We expect hospital admissions with those suffering from

ADS to increase further and would like to request that anyone with more minor health issues treat them as best they can at home. To limit spread of the virus, no visitors will be permitted in hospitals until further notice. We advise those over the age of sixty-five who are currently showing no symptoms of ADS to remain in their homes for the next several days."

The press deluged both doctors with questions, so the microbiologist added that hospitals hadn't diagnosed anyone under sixty-five with the virus but that it was possible people with weak immune systems could be more likely to catch it. "Everyone, regardless of age, should perform frequent and thorough hand-washing," he said sternly. "The elderly and anyone with compromised immune systems should wear an N95 mask when out of their homes as a precautionary measure." So far, the only good news was that the virus hadn't killed anyone.

Mom and I remained silent during the conference. Only afterwards did she turn to me and say, "They'll devote all their resources to this now. It's just a matter of time until they come up with a treatment."

"But what about Dad — will he still be able to fly over?"

Mom curved her arm affectionately around me, leaning in to my side. "Of course he will. It's only an advisory. They're not suspending flights. I just wish I could see your gran and granddad."

I wondered if she was afraid they'd forget her completely. What if they had ADS for the rest of their lives? Would they have to stay in the hospital forever?

"Can we call Dad again?" I asked, checking my watch.

It was almost nine o'clock in the morning in Kingston.

Mom went off to speak with him from behind her closed bedroom door first. When it was my turn to talk to him, Dad said he'd booked a flight for tomorrow night, which meant he'd arrive on Friday morning — only two days' time. "So I'll be there for your birthday after all," he added.

My birthday barbecue was supposed to be on Saturday, but I couldn't imagine having it without my grandparents. After I got off the phone more calls came in, one from Aunt Fiona and another from Uncle Declan in Australia, who'd heard about the advisory on the radio.

I'd never been good at doing nothing, and I got restless waiting for Mom to get off the phone. Twenty minutes later my brain was still running wild, like a race car driver with miles of open road ahead. I tiptoed into the kitchen, caught Mom's eye, and signaled to the door.

She covered the phone with her hand and listened to me ask, "Can I go out and rollerblade?" There weren't many ice rinks in Dublin, and I always ended up missing being on the ice. Blading wasn't quite the same, but at least you could do it on any old strip of pavement.

"Just on the street here where I can see you," Mom replied.

I laced up as fast as I could and hurtled up the sidewalk and back. Someone's calico cat was lurking by a bush near the end of the street. It stared sulkily at me as I whizzed past, like I was invading its territory. Then I saw Ciara leaving her house with her dad and Adam. She called me over and said her dad was taking her to get her hair trimmed. "And then we're going round to my gran's place to make sure she's not getting sick," she added. "Can you believe that about the virus? I know we've been talking about it a lot yesterday and today, but I thought … I don't know …"

That we were letting our imaginations go crazy and that whatever was really happening wasn't serious enough to have a press conference about? There was a part of me that had thought that too, even after all the weird things that'd happened.

"It's like something that would happen at the beginning of a movie," I said breathlessly. "Like when Gwyneth Paltrow got sick in *Contagion* before the virus turned into a global plague and started killing millions of people."

Ciara crossed her arms in front of her and shivered. "The Spanish flu killed over fifty million people about a hundred years ago. They said so on the news."

Mr. Kavanagh and Adam were already sitting in the car, and at that point Mr. Kavanagh rolled down the window and stared at us with somber eyes. "Okay, stop freaking each other out," he lectured. "No one's died, and this isn't a Gwyneth Paltrow movie. Ciara, get in the car. We have to go."

Ciara said she'd talk to me later. I turned and started skating again, the sound of the car fading into the distance. I wished I had my hockey stick and a puck too. I wished I were on ice, someone speeding towards my net — that would stop me from thinking about anything else for a while.

But no such luck. Instead a woman crouched in the bushes ahead, diligently planting forks and spoons into the soil so that the stems of the cutlery stuck up. She had curly gray hair, and she waved when she saw me. I automatically waved back.

Maybe there was a good reason she was filling up her garden with forks and spoons. But when you saw someone planting cutlery and you'd just heard there was an outbreak of something called amnestic-delirium syndrome, the virus seemed the likeliest cause. I'd passed the woman by then, but I turned fast, skating back towards her. Not all the way, because I remembered Mrs. Redmond's frying pan, but closer. "Are you all right?" I asked, a weird brightness to my voice, like I'd swallowed a bottle of self-tanning lotion.

"I like the green and the sky," she said, smiling as she struggled to hold back a cough. "Do I know you?" She reached down to straighten a fork, her eyes flicking back to my face. "I don't seem to know anybody anymore. I used to, but ..." She shrugged. "Everything's gone now, isn't it?"

The woman didn't seem angry like Mrs. Redmond or even my grandfather when he'd banged the counter and argued with my mother about my uncles. "Not everything," I replied slowly. "The sky and the grass are still here."

"Yes." The woman's smile reached her eyebrows, making me feel as though I'd somehow managed to say the exact right thing. "That's true."

She was still grinning as I turned away. I began skating straight back to my gran and granddad's house, refusing to turn my head in the direction of a tall man in striped pajamas who'd just stepped out of a house across the street. He was making his way tentatively down the driveway as

I surged past, and with a start I realized that he looked the same age as my father. Not over sixty like Deirdre Redmond, Father Mahoney, my grandparents, or the woman planting cutlery, but still infected. I would've bet on it.

They hadn't been exaggerating on the news. If anything, they'd been downplaying the spread of the virus. From what I could see, ADS was everywhere, and you didn't need to be a senior citizen to get it.

SIX

MOM CALLED THE police to tell them about the wandering man in his pajamas and the spoon- and fork-planting woman. The cops said they'd try to send someone to our street but that with so many reports of strange incidences it'd be hours before they could get here.

Mom repeated all that for me after she'd gotten off the phone, and said we should stay indoors — no more blading for me. But there was one thing I knew I could do. I scoured the living room cabinets until I found a thick spiral notebook that had never been written in.

What if I got sick too? What if I forgot everyone I knew just like the woman outside in her front yard? They'd all forget me too, probably. What if, in the end, none of us remembered and so there'd be no one to remind us?

Feverishly, I began to write. Everything, everything, everything I could think of. A complete record of all the important events that had occurred since I'd arrived in Dublin five days earlier. My nerves jerked across each page, making twenty percent of the words practically illegible.

After I'd caught up with the things that had happened so far, I made a list. My dad made lists of stuff to do for the café all the time. They helped him remember. Kept him organized.

So, what did I need to remember about me? For the second time, I started at the very beginning.

MY EARLIEST MEMORIES

- Skating on my grandfather's homemade ice rink (at 3), never wanting to stop.
- Sitting in a steamy bathroom with my dad when I had a bad cough (maybe 4).
- Riding a pony on a farm when I was 3, the smell of hay tickling my nostrils.
- Crying at Mom's friend's house (at 3 1/2 or 4) because I was too young to be allowed to play with the daughter's guinea pig. In the end, they let me hold it for ten seconds.
- Mom reading to me, but from lots of different books so it must be a bunch of memories jumbled up into one. In some of the memories, it's my dad reading.

Finally, it was time to go to bed, and I set down my pen. The police never came, and during the night I began to hear noises. Not the usual creaking ones from inside the house but freaky ones from out on the street that were too loud to ignore. Snatches of shouts and strange banging noises. I tiptoed to the bedroom window and froze at the pane. A crowd of people had gathered like a loose mob; half the street must have been outside. Some of them were talking to each other in raised voices and others were in their own worlds, not speaking to anyone. Not one of them looked what you would call calm or composed. They were all either wild or dazed.

One bald man in a tennis shirt and Nike sweatpants was going from house to house, pounding agitatedly on each door. A round woman in a burgundy robe and slippers was attempting to break into someone's black Mini Cooper with a golf club and a pair of scissors. Maybe it was even *her* car. Maybe she had the key but didn't remember where it was. If she could've gotten inside the car I bet she wouldn't have remembered where she wanted to go either.

Mom rushed into the room and put her arm protectively around me in the dark. "Come away from the window, Naomi. I'm going to ring the guards. They need to take care of this."

She led me into her bedroom, where I sat on the bed with her while she tried to get through to the police on the phone. Each time their line was busy and she had to hang up and hit redial. While she was doing it, a thump at the front door made us both jump in our skin. The bald man making his rounds. He'd struck the door with such force that it wouldn't have surprised me if he'd used his fist and made his knuckles bleed.

"You keep trying," Mom said, handing me the phone. "I'm going to have another look outside."

I couldn't get through either. Alone in Mom's bedroom I listened to the *beep beep beep* and hoped I was dreaming. Things like this didn't happen in real life.

But I didn't wake up, and the police didn't answer. Mom slipped back into the room with me and said, "We're okay, Naomi. Even if the guards can't get to us. I don't think any of these people are dangerous. They're just in a muddle."

And angry and lost. Outside, a car engine started and a dog barked. Ripley? I ran to my bedroom to get my cell and call Ciara. There was no answer from her either. I reeled back to my mom's room with my cell in my hand. Mom had managed to reach someone, but the way she was talking I knew it wasn't the cops.

"Dad?" I asked her.

She shook her head. "Fiona. They haven't seen anything like this, being out in the country like they are, but she's switched on the news and there's trouble all over Dublin, Cork, and other urban centers."

My cell rang in my closed fist. I flipped over the phone, saw Shehan's name, and answered it. "The whole street's gone mad," he said, his voice high-pitched like it had been before it'd changed.

"We can't get through to the police on the phone." I chewed my lip. "We've tried and tried." Outside, anguished cries rang out and glass shattered. I pictured a million shards glittering in the street, the crowd walking through them in their bare feet, trailing blood. "Did you hear that?" My ears and fingertips tingled. "They've broken something."

I wasn't so sure that Mom was right about the sick not being dangerous. Some of them seemed completely unhinged.

"The only thing I can hear now is some old fella shouting himself hoarse," Shehan said. "Whatever it was must be closer to you."

I peered out my mom's bedroom window, searching out

the cause of the noise. All I could see from where I was standing was the darkened backyard, and I dashed back to my own bedroom to check from that window too. "What are you and your dad going to do?" I asked, unable to see any broken glass from either spot, just the unruly crowd milling around in the street below.

"Dad's downstairs watching the chaos on the news. I reckon we'll just sit tight. What else can anyone do? There are too many of them."

Way too many to bring to the hospital ourselves, and I was sure some of them wouldn't have let us take them. "My dad's flying in Friday morning." His flight was scheduled to leave at 8:55 p.m. Toronto time and arrive at Dublin airport at 8:30 in the morning Ireland time. "I can't wait until he gets here. Not like it will change anything, but still ..."

"It'll be tomorrow before we know it," Shehan said.

I held my phone away from me to check the time. It was 2:47 a.m., which meant there were roughly thirty hours until Dad would get here. It felt like a long, long time. I wasn't sure how we'd get through the night, even. I definitely wouldn't be able to sleep knowing all those people were outside in the street, a virus destroying their identities.

Suddenly my grandparents seemed like the lucky ones in comparison, safe in their hospital beds. Who knew what would become of everyone else?

DAY SEVEN

Thursday morning came quietly. The noise had died away sometime during the dead of night, and I'd fallen asleep in Mom's bed, her speaking to my dad next to me with the lamp on. As soon as I woke up to daylight I checked the clock again: 7:27. Twenty-five hours until Dad would be in Dublin with us.

Mom was still asleep as I padded into my room and stared down at the street. Several front doors had been left wide open, the black Mini's paint job had been scratched within an inch of its life, and two fuzzy purple slippers lay abandoned in the middle of the road. If it weren't for a couple of birds singing it would have been completely quiet. The only person in view was a woman sitting gloomily by the curb, her lips moving like she was talking to herself. Her hair was a tangled pitch black, and she didn't look much older than my mother, making her the second ADS-infected person I'd seen who wasn't a senior citizen.

Ignoring how early it was, I called Ciara. She picked up on the fourth ring, the two of us starting to talk at the exact same time. Usually that was something that made me laugh. Not today. Ciara told me that her dad had gone out and tried to talk sense to some of the infected people, but no one had listened to him. Then the man who'd been pounding on doors had charged over with a red face and started poking Mr. Kavanagh in the chest, asking if he was responsible for what was happening.

"He followed Dad back to our house and kept slamming himself against the door," she said. "You wouldn't believe how strong he was. I was so scared he'd get in. But eventually he got tired and wandered off."

No wonder Ciara hadn't heard her phone ring when I'd called last night. "They're all gone now," I said. "There's just one woman left out there on the street."

"They have some kind of roving SWAT teams out there scooping up groups of sick people," Ciara said soberly. "I saw it on the news before I fell asleep. Maybe they got them."

"I hope so. I don't want them to come back." I felt cold at the thought.

The best news was that Ciara's grandmother didn't seem to be sick. After seeing so many older people in the street the night before, I'd been starting to think they all had ADS. Ciara and I agreed to check in with each other later, and I hung up and put together a breakfast of toast coated in marmalade. Then it was only twenty-four hours until my dad's arrival. A day wasn't long, no matter how I'd felt about it the night before. Especially now that no one was yelling outside, trying to break into cars or pounding on doors. That's what I told myself.

When Mom got up she made more phone calls — to my uncles, Aunt Fiona, and Dad — and then, as a precaution, we drove to the nearest supermarket to stock up on food and emergency supplies. The local Tesco was about halfway down Haverhill Road, but it took lots longer than usual to get there because we had to steer around a series of abandoned cars. Finally, it became such an obstacle course that we couldn't drive any farther and had to park the car in the middle of the street and walk the rest of the way.

The police were watching over the grocery store, making sure everyone kept the peace, and we had to stand in line for a long time to get inside. While we were waiting, a middle-aged man with dark circles under his eyes lumbered towards the line. "What an ugly lot!" he shouted angrily at the gathered group of us. "I can't stand the sight and stink of you." He stalked close to me and my mom — near enough that I could smell his meaty-stale breath. Mom pulled me close to her and the man hobbled on, gnashing his teeth and grunting. Two cops grabbed him and began pulling him away from the supermarket. The man threw his jaws open and bit one of them on the cheek. Blood spilled from the police officer's face as they continued to drag the man away.

Digging your teeth into someone like that was something usually only animals did, and seeing it happen right in front of me made my ears ring and my breath speed up. Everyone waiting was instantly more nervous. Other infected came and went, the police chasing away the ones who got too close and ignoring the others. When it was our turn to go into the store we found the shelves half empty and had to hurry up and down each of the aisles gathering items in our arms because all the carts and baskets were in use. Mom was happy that at least they had N95 masks in stock and grabbed one each for me, her, and Dad.

Once we'd arrived back at the car there were so many others parked behind it that Mom had to steer the car over the curb to get around the rest of them, like she was a stunt driver in an action movie.

"I hope I don't wreck the car," Mom said lightly. "Your gran and granddad wouldn't be very pleased with me, would they?"

My lungs filled up with nervous laughter that bubbled into the air. Mom broke into a smile as the car's two right wheels landed securely back on the street and she coasted over to the left lane. Before long we were back at my grandparents' house, unloading our things from the supermarket and then settling down on the couch to watch the news.

Countless fires were raging across the country (mostly from stoves left on), and every supermarket open for business had been overrun with customers and surrounded by police, just like the one we'd been inside earlier. People had begun to panic in reaction to the number of ADS-infected abandoning their homes and acting disruptively. Meanwhile, gridlock and high demand was making it impossible for emergency services to reach everyone who needed them. The hospitals were packed to overflowing with ADS patients.

And that was just the beginning. The two o'clock press conference following the news was grimmer. The Chief Medical Officer himself had taken ill, and the microbiologist said that some people in their forties and fifties had been admitted to hospitals around the country. "I should stress that we're not seeing any deaths from ADS, and none of the patients have developed pneumonia or any other serious physical issues. The main symptoms are profound memory loss and confused thinking. Some people currently infected with the virus already suffered from dementia, but many others had no previous cognitive issues whatsoever. We're not yet certain if people under forty may also be susceptible to amnestic-delirium syndrome, but at this time the government have decided to take extraordinary measures to prevent the spread of what's proving to be an extremely aggressive virus."

The microbiologist explained that the Taoiseach — that's the elected Irish head of government — had also been stricken with ADS. It was one of his cabinet ministers who took the podium to announce the government was ordering a ten o'clock curfew. "We also have a responsibility to the international community to halt the spread of this virus, and after speaking with the World Health Organization and the British Prime Minister's Office, we have jointly decided to temporarily suspend all travel to and from Northern Ireland and the Republic of Ireland. As of two p.m. today, flights and ferries in and out of Ireland and Northern Ireland have been halted."

I didn't hear what the cabinet minister said after that. There was a big whoosh inside my head. *Dad won't make it. We're stuck here, and he can't make it. We're alone in this.*

Mom coughed next to me. The sound was what brought me back and got me listening again, not to the TV but to her. She saw me staring and made a dismissive motion with her hand. "It's dry in here," she said. "That's all."

Ireland wasn't dry *anywhere*. The air was always humid. My dad had once told me that was why the salt clumped in the shakers here.

"Don't look at me like that," Mom said. "I haven't forgotten a thing."

I tuned back in to the press conference. There had to be some good news mixed in with the bad. The cabinet minister was explaining that except in cases of clear emergency, people should remain in their homes. The motorways had been closed to all but emergency personnel, and the closure would be enforced by the police and the Irish army. Since there was currently no treatment for the virus, family members were advised to keep ADS sufferers at home for the next three days while larger treatment centers were set up.

The microbiologist returned to the podium to stress that anyone interacting with an ADS sufferer should be wearing an N95 mask, and frequent disinfecting of household surfaces was crucial. There would be another conference on Saturday morning to list the newly established treatment centers.

The reporters began to bark out questions, and I turned to look at Mom. Her skin seemed sallow. It could've just been the light. Her long fingers were trembling slightly in her lap. She locked them together to keep them still.

"Mom, what's Saturday?" I asked, my own fingers as icy as ten blue popsicles.

"What do you mean *what's Saturday?*" she asked. "Are you testing me? I'm fine, Naomi, trust me. We'll do like they advised on the news and stay inside for the next few days until they can get things under control and we'll be fine. I know we're both really disappointed about your dad not being able to fly in, but we can talk to him every day on the phone."

"I know." I pressed my lips shut and nodded. "But what's Saturday? What *day* is it?"

Mom dragged one of her fingers across her right eyebrow. There was a faraway look in her eyes. "I'm sorry we won't be able to have your party now. We'll do it when things get back to normal."

I couldn't have cared less about the party, presents, or anything else; I was just happy she hadn't forgotten the fact that Saturday was my birthday. She'd passed my test.

SEVEN

MY DAD WAS even more upset than we were that he couldn't fly to Dublin to be with us. I stayed strong on the phone with him, telling myself there was no reason to be afraid because all of this would be over soon, and then Dad, Uncle Declan, and Uncle Mark would be here. My grandparents too. They'd be cured of amnestic-delirium syndrome, and the hospital would send them home. We'd have a big barbecue and sit around talking about how crazy this time had been.

That's what I kept saying to myself Thursday night.

DAY EIGHT

I said the same again on Friday morning and afternoon. Outside it was mostly quiet, but from time to time I heard sirens in the distance. I ignored Mom's cough and the little things she'd started to forget. Things like Ciara's name or what we'd eaten for lunch. They were things she remembered later anyway, things that didn't matter.

Next were bigger things and longer gaps before she remembered again. In the evening, she forgot Dad wasn't with us. I came out of the bathroom and found her walking through the house searching for him. One look at my face as we met in the hallway and she realized her mistake. "I'm sorry," she said, wrapping her arms around me and hugging me close. "Let's call your dad."

She put on a mask first and made me put one on too. "We should wear them whenever we're in the same room," she advised.

I talked to my dad for longer than she did because he was afraid Mom might forget what he told her. The first thing was that we needed to call Aunt Fiona so that we could all deal with this together. The second thing was that Dad was going to call for updates three times a day but that I should call him whenever anything new happened. Lastly, he wanted me to talk to my mom non-stop about our lives and everything that'd been going on with the virus in the hopes that she'd be able to hang on longer that way.

Just before I hung up, Dad furrowed his brow and said, "You're a brave girl, Naomi. You always have been. You do all those things I told you, and I'll talk to you again before bed. I love you, sweetie."

I told Dad I loved him too, and when I got off the phone I noticed Mom sitting at the table in the kitchen, furiously scribbling on a piece of long lined paper.

"What're you writing?" I asked.

Mom didn't stop to look up. "You were the one who gave me the idea when I saw you writing yesterday." I dashed to the table and bent over her work. She'd already jotted down four paragraphs about our lives in the style of a Wikipedia entry. "It's so that if I forget, I'll have this to remind me," she admitted, finally pausing to look up at me.

A bruise formed in my throat. Suddenly I felt like her mother instead of vice versa. I forced my words out into the open, and they slashed at my already sore throat. "Dad says we should call Aunt Fiona and figure out how we can all be together."

"I'll do it right away," Mom said, handing me the paper and pen as she slid the chair away from the table. I took her place, continuing my record of events until my hand smarted. Flexing my fingers, I jotted down a master list for my mom. If her memory failed, it might be easier to read a list than a bunch of paragraphs.

MOM: THINGS YOU NEED TO KNOW
- Gran & Granddad are in the hospital with ADS (memory sickness). That's why they aren't here with us.
- So far there is no cure, but ADS doesn't kill people.
- We don't live at 47 Sykes Close full-time. We just visit in summers.
- Dad is back home in Kingston because of his café and because right now the Irish borders are closed so other people won't get sick too.
- If there's an emergency you should call your sister, Fiona, (her number is in your phone and also Gran's red address book in the kitchen) or Mr. & Mrs. Kavanagh from down the road (also in the book).
- Your brothers, Declan & Mark, are supposed to come for a visit from Australia at the end of the month, but I guess that depends on the borders.
- You met Dad on a date your friend Denise set you up on. You said you liked his laugh but the restaurant was

horrible. A tiny hair was in your calamari.
- Your favorite movie is *Amélie* and your favorite musician is Prince.

I didn't scribble down that Prince had died. There was so much bad news already, and if Mom forgot he was dead, I didn't want to be the one to remind her.

Mom talked to Aunt Fiona while I continued to write. From the start I could hear that the news was bad. Uncle Brendan was sick. Aunt Fiona had chills and was having trouble following conversations, so she thought she was too. They couldn't come get us, and since the two of them were infected and contagious, they didn't think they should be around me anyway.

Out of all of us, it seemed I was the only one who didn't have the virus. Probably I'd be next to catch it. I silently began quizzing myself, running through my teammates' names and then special dates, like my friends' birthdays and Mom and Dad's anniversary. I didn't want to forget who I was. I didn't want to forget *anything*, and so far I hadn't.

Was my throat dry? Was I holding back a cough? I didn't think so.

I wrote out another list to stop my mind from spinning out of control. More things I wanted to make sure I remembered.

MY HOCKEY TEAMMATES
- Alexis Hebert — my best friend since she moved to Kingston in fifth grade because we can tell each other

everything and even if one of us is in a bad mood we can usually make each other smile.

- Lily Lam — tough and calm. You can never panic when Lily's around, she won't let you. She's one of my closest friends.
- Taneisha Frazier — our top scorer and another one of my closest friends. She won the seventh grade science fair award too.
- Anna Khachatryan — mostly quiet and then every once in a while she says something funny out of the blue that completely cracks everyone up.
- Lena Clark — total team player.
- Winnie Anderson — has played baseball, volleyball, and soccer too. She's the kind of person who can do everything well.
- Talia David — hates being the smallest person on the team and works super hard to make up for it.
- Noor Choudhary — probably the nicest person on the team. Really supportive and cheers you up if you're having a bad day.
- Gracelyn Maddocks — kind of a puck hog.
- Megan Rich — her parents let her get a tattoo of her cat on her arm after it died.
- Scarlet Belanger — brags about her fifteen-year-old boyfriend a lot. Half the team roll their eyes when they look away after she mentions him.
- Rowan Williams — a better goalie than she thinks she is. We all keep telling her that to help her confidence catch up.
- Evi Lewandowski — trained as a figure skater for years

too so she's fantastic on the ice.

- Davina Rieder — quit hockey halfway through the season when she got a concussion. A player on another team sent her headfirst into the boards. It was pretty awful.
- Kasey Georgiou — smells like cinnamon (because she chews gum non-stop) and never lies.
- Christina Nikolyukin — has such white blond hair and is even taller than me and super strong. She basically looks like a Viking.

I couldn't imagine forgetting any of my teammates, but probably people sick with ADS, or who had regular dementia before all this happened, couldn't have imagined forgetting either.

Scared as I was about Mom being sick, I was relieved that I was okay so far. As long as I stayed that way, it meant I could look out for her. That's what I told Dad when he called again before bedtime, that I'd just keep repeating everything over and over for her. Not give her a chance to forget. Then we could just stay here together until they found a cure.

I'd been so distracted with sticking close to Mom for the entire day that I'd barely had a chance to look at my text messages. Earlier there'd been a couple from Alexis and Lily and one from Taneisha, each of them wondering how Mom and I were doing. It wasn't until I went up to bed that I spied my phone on the bedside table and checked new messages.

Ciara and Shehan had both texted to check up on me.

They'd been shut up in their houses since Thursday's press conference. Ciara's text said she'd wanted to come see me but that her parents wouldn't let her and didn't want her tying up our landline, which should be left free for emergencies. It was too late to call Ciara, so I texted her about my mom being sick. Then I texted Shehan, whose message had said his father had a cough and that he'd gone very quiet. It sounded like what'd happened to my gran, which wasn't good. I told Shehan about my dad's idea of repeating essential facts aloud for my mom and also that I'd written a list of things down on a piece of paper for her.

Shehan texted back straight away. "How do you feel?"

"No fever and no cough," I replied. "Are you okay?"

"I'm not sick either," he texted. "Keep in touch. We need to stick together."

"I will. You too!" That was the final thing I keyed in before my head hit the pillow. I had weirdly vivid dreams all night. In the last one I was flying over rooftops and trees, staring down at a horde of people who didn't know who they were. Some of them were shouting at me and waving their fists. The dream seemed to go on for hours until the scene morphed into a hockey arena. I was standing in front of a net with no padding on as Alexis, in full hockey gear, broke away from the game action and skated over to me.

"What are you doing?" she yelled. "You're supposed to be in Ireland making sure your mom doesn't forget."

She was right.

DAY NINE

I woke with a start. The sky outside was a shade of gray that made it impossible to tell what time it was, and the radio next to me was flashing 12:00. The power must've failed and come back on. I threw my hand out to reach for my cell.

8:14 a.m. A cellphone rang in the distance as I tossed off the covers and stood. Dad?

Normally I wouldn't have barged into Mom's room without knocking, but I didn't want us to miss his call. I burst inside to see Mom sitting up in bed, staring blankly at her phone on the nightstand. "Pick it up!" I yelled. "It's probably Dad."

Mom's right hand floated tentatively through the air, almost like it wasn't attached to her. She closed her fingers around the phone and lifted it to her ear. "Hello?" Her voice sounded as if it were full of holes. Some essence of her had leaked out of her body.

My heart sank. She was worse today. I saw it in her eyes too. She didn't recognize my father's voice over the phone. "Give it to me," I said, striding over to rip the phone from Mom's hand. I quickly switched the call to FaceTime.

"Naomi?" Dad cried, stubble poking out from his chin and cheeks. "Your mom wouldn't talk to me."

"She's sicker." It hurt to say.

Meanwhile, Mom was standing, looking down at her legs like the shape or size of them under her nightgown was somehow wrong. She began to inch towards the door, moving with the carefulness of someone who wasn't sure what they wanted or where they were.

I glanced desperately around for the pieces of paper we'd written the facts of our lives down on last night. We must have left them on the kitchen table.

"Wait!" I shouted, tossing the phone down on the bed. "You don't recognize me, do you? It's Naomi, Mom. You're sick. That's why you don't remember." I began explaining about my grandparents, ADS, and Dad being home in Kingston.

Mom's cheeks hollowed out as she listened to my words. "I'm sorry," she said quietly. "I don't remember any of that."

"Or me?"

Mom pulled her chin towards her chest. "Or you." She coughed, one of her palms flying to her face to cover it.

It's weird the things people remember the longest. How to use the telephone and that old polite thing about covering your mouth with your hand when you cough. That was the complete wrong thing to do, it turned out, because it helped spread the germs when the sick person touched something afterwards. My science teacher, Mr. Nishiada, told my class that.

My mom didn't remember it was the wrong thing, and she didn't remember me. She waved her hands in front of her face as though she was trying to fight her way through a fog. "It can't be true," she said, advancing forward again. "I'm not old enough to have a daughter."

"You are. I'm her." I followed her into the hall. "Mom, where are you going?"

"Stop calling me that," she said. "I don't *know* you."

"Why would I lie to you?" But she wouldn't even swivel to watch the words come out of my mouth. She continued down the stairs and then slowly through each of the rooms: the formal front room where my gran and granddad seldom sat, the combination living/dining room where they usually spent most of their time, and, finally, the eat-in kitchen where Mom plucked the sheets of lined paper from the table.

"We wrote those," I told her. "You did the first page, and then I made the list so you would *know* things even if you forgot."

Mom crossed her arms tightly in front of her and shivered. "This is my parents' house. It looks … changed. But this is it. We're in Dublin, aren't we?"

I hadn't noticed so much when she'd first started speaking, but her Irish accent had grown stronger, the decades spent in Canada erased from her voice.

I nodded and pointed to the papers. "Have you read it all?"

Mom untangled her arms to wipe her forehead with the back of her hand. "It's warm in here," she complained. That must have been because of the low-grade fever the microbiologist had said was an ADS symptom. "Look, I'm sorry I don't remember you. I think you must be mistaking me for someone else. Like I said, I'm not old enough to be a mother."

I shouldn't have been angry with her. She couldn't help it if she couldn't remember. That was the way ADS worked. But something inside me felt she should've fought harder not to forget me, and I took her hand in mine and tugged her into the living room with me. She didn't fight me, but she scowled like a teenage girl.

I marched her in front of the mantelpiece, where a gilded mirror hung, and pointed at our image. Mom was only a couple of inches taller than me. We had the same mouth, same chin, and near enough to the same coloring.

"You're plenty old enough," I snapped. "You're my mother. I was born during a tropical storm back in Kingston. Dad was afraid the two of you wouldn't make it to the hospital. The roads were so bad that he said it was like driving underwater."

Mom folded a hand under her chin as she continued to stare at herself in shock. Her mouth jolted open twice before she brought herself to say, "What's your name?"

"Naomi." My voice rasped, rebelling at having to tell my own mother my name. "Naomi Seiler."

Mom drifted towards the couch, pulling her legs up onto the couch with her. It was funny to see her sit that way — like we were the same age. I flicked on the TV and then sat down in my granddad's chair, channel surfing until I hit Irish news. "This will explain more about what's happening."

According to the broadcast, several new treatment centers would open tomorrow, including ones inside sporting arenas and concert/exhibition venues like the 3Arena in downtown Dublin, the RDS main hall, and the National Basketball Arena. There was no treatment or cure yet. Doctors were trying to stop the spread of ADS and keep infected patients calm to prevent them from being a danger. People in their thirties had begun to show signs of infection, but so far no children or young people had been stricken. That aside, the only positive news was that there'd been no signs of widespread infection outside Ireland. Only two patients — one in Manchester and one in Copenhagen — had confirmed cases of ADS. Both of them had recently returned from Ireland and were being kept in strict isolation.

I left the news on for Mom while I rushed into the hall to grab the cordless and call my dad back from the landline. That was how it went for most of the day: Mom in front of the TV absorbing the news as I continually reminded her who she was and who I was. She didn't remember for herself, but she seemed to trust me and what I was telling her.

Every few hours Dad called or texted to see how we were doing. All day I had a lump in my throat the size of a marble. All day I was scared that I'd develop a cough or Mom would turn angry in her confusion. At one point I took a book of Victorian poetry off the living room shelf and made Mom read poems aloud to me at the kitchen table while I browned some beef in a pan and boiled carrots and cauliflower. I only knew how to cook some basic things, but I didn't trust Mom near the stove. Plus, I was hoping the poetry would help connect her to who she really was — an English teacher, someone who loved words and stories. I wasn't really listening to Mom read as I prepared the food, but I heard her stop with a gasp at the end of a poem by Emily Dickinson.

I twirled to look at her. Mom was no longer looking at

the book — she was reciting from memory as she gazed into my eyes.

> If I can stop one heart from breaking,
> I shall not live in vain;
> If I can ease one life the aching,
> Or cool one pain,
> Or help one fainting robin
> Unto his nest again,
> I shall not live in vain.

The beef sizzled in the pan as warmth flooded my body. I opened my mouth and spluttered, "You know it, don't you? You *remember* it."

The clouds had gone from Mom's eyes. "I remember," she confirmed. "I remember everything." She jumped up from her chair and bolted towards me. One of her hands smoothed my hair. "I'm so sorry, Naomi." She hopped back from me as quickly as she'd approached, dread stretching across her cheeks. "Where are the masks?"

"You wouldn't keep yours on." She'd kept forgetting its purpose and yanking it off. Seeing mine had seemed to scare her, so I'd given up on that too. I'd been afraid to do anything that might chase her away.

"Are you still all right?" Mom asked, maintaining her distance.

I nodded eagerly. "I'm okay. No one young has it. We just have to wait it out here until they find a cure." I said it with more certainty than I felt. I had no idea how long it could take to develop a cure or vaccine. But the world couldn't abandon us, could they? Someone would have to do something. Sweep in and save us.

Mom coughed into her sleeve and took another two steps back. "I have to call your father and Fiona. Before ..." She let the unsaid words dangle. *Before she forgot again.* Her eyes were sad and apologetic. "And the government must be doing something about the children with sick parents. I should make some calls about that too, and —"

"I'm not going anywhere," I interrupted. "I'm staying with you."

Mom's bottom lip quivered. She shook her head as though what I was suggesting was impossible.

"Sit down and eat first," I added. "The food will get cold."

Mom obeyed me and sat herself at the table. I dished out the food and poured us each a glass of milk, talking at her all the while so she wouldn't forget. I tried to sit down next to her, but Mom waved me away. "Not so close," she said, getting up to move towards the counter. "You sit. I'll eat it over here, and as soon as we're done, I'm calling your dad."

It was so good to see her taking charge that I smiled. "Okay."

We ate quickly. I wasn't hungry but forced myself to finish every bite; I needed to keep as well and strong as possible.

It was when I'd eaten the last carrot and put down my fork that I saw the change in Mom's face. She stopped chewing and glared at me.

"We're in your parents' house," I said quickly. "You had to take them to the hospital a few days ago. It's a sickness, a virus. It's making everyone forget. You too." I snatched up the same papers from before — the ones that explained.

Mom wouldn't even look at them. Her eyes were as dark as the bottom of the ocean.

"Sit down," I told her. "Please." I stumbled over my words as I continued to tell her about our situation, and every second she looked as though she wanted to bolt. I didn't know how much longer I could do this; it was exhausting. Tears welled up behind my eyes and down the length of my throat. "*Stay with me*. I'll turn on the TV and show you the news. Then you'll know what's happening."

Mom swallowed whatever morsel of food was left in her mouth. In seconds she was walking through the kitchen door and into the hall. I followed, grabbing at her arm. "Mom, where are you going? Come into the living room."

Mom's eyes shrunk as she turned to take in my image. "I'm not your mother. *Don't call me that*. I don't know you." She shoved her feet into a pair of running shoes she found near the front door. I doubt she specifically remembered them, but they happened to be hers.

"Where are you going?" I shouted. "It's not safe outside. We have to stay in the house."

"I don't have to do anything," Mom said, pulling away from me. "Leave me alone." She pushed the door open and broke into a sprint. There was no time to put on my own shoes or close the door. I stumbled after her through the street, bare feet raw on the pavement. If she'd remembered me she'd know she couldn't get away — I was quicker, even without shoes. Or I would have been, if my heel hadn't caught on some unseen slippery thing, knocking me onto my back on the hard cement. The fall knocked the wind out of me and scraped the skin on my right arm. I didn't have a second to waste; Mom already had a healthy lead. I staggered to my feet, ignoring the stinging sensation in my arm, and followed my mother around the corner onto Birchwood Street.

EIGHT

UP AHEAD A bald man with a wispy beard and torn sweater sat in the middle of the sidewalk with an open copy of the Yellow Pages spread out in front of him, like he was reading it from cover to cover. After seeing one of the infected bite a police officer with such brutality that he'd drawn blood, there was no way I was getting anywhere near the man, and he chuckled heartily as I took to the grass to run around him. "Catch her!" he shouted after me. "She's getting away."

He had a laugh that repeated like bad indigestion; it didn't sound funny at all. So far I couldn't see anyone else, except Mom. She'd hit Haverhill Road in seconds, and then it would be easier to lose track of her. I had to catch up.

In the distance I heard traffic noises and shouting. Mom veered to the left, onto the main street that cut through Haverhill and connected it with downtown Dublin. The last time I'd been on Haverhill Road its lower half had looked like a parking lot. The way the road curved made it impossible for me to see whether cars still blocked its way in the distance. At my end the road remained mostly clear, and a convoy of four double-decker city buses hunkered with their engines running while groups of soldiers in gas masks swarmed in front of them. The soldiers were armed with semi-automatic weapons, and my instinct was to steer clear of them, tear back in the direction I'd come. But Mom was running full tilt towards the cluster of uniforms.

I was close enough to hear her shout, "What's happening? Are we at war?"

"Get on the bus, missus," one of the taller soldiers commanded. "We're evacuating." I was surprised that I could hear him fine through the gas mask. Mom slowed to glance at the bus. I looked at it too, my legs still in motion. It was yellow and blue, with the same Dublin bus logo I'd seen on every local bus. The sight was familiar, but the context was all wrong. The bus's top deck teemed with people, and while some of the men and women sitting inside with their faces pressed against the window seemed afraid, others just looked angry. Two soldiers stood on either side of the bus's front door as yet more people filed inside.

The soldier who'd addressed my mother reached out to grab for her arm. It was the soldier beside him who glanced over his shoulder, saw me coming, and yelled, "Stop!"

I froze on the spot, every inch of me except my right arm, which pointed automatically at my mother. "That's my mom. Let her go."

The first soldier, the tall one, had an iron grip on my mother that he didn't loosen. "We're not going to hurt her. We're escorting people to the medical base at the RDS.

Anyone infected. They need to be off the streets and in quarantine."

"They said on the news to keep them at home if you could," I reminded him, defiance settling into my spine.

"Which you haven't managed," the tall soldier said dispassionately. "She needs to get on the bus. End of discussion." Mom had begun to struggle like a child, twisting her body left and right but without any real strength.

Behind us someone screamed. I turned to see a blond man in a sweatshirt and cargo pants being tased by one of the many other soldiers. The blond man fell to the ground like a tree zapped in a thunderstorm. Two soldiers lifted him, carrying him towards the bus.

"Sedation here!" the soldier holding on to Mom called. A female soldier with a syringe jabbed Mom's arm. Mom went limp, her legs beginning to buckle under her. The male soldier lifted her into his arms, me tagging along after him.

"You can't do this," I told him. "I'll look after her."

"Look after yourself," he said, striding forward to hand Mom to someone inside the bus, as though she were nothing more than a FedEx delivery.

One of the soldiers standing by the bus door put a hand up to stop me from following. "Not you," he said.

The tall soldier, now empty-handed, stood back and stared at me. "How old are you?" he asked. "Do you have somewhere to go? The churches and schools are taking in children who don't have anyone to look after them." He motioned to the bus parked directly behind the one we were standing nearest to.

Maybe it sounds crazy, but I thought if I got on that bus I might never see my mother again. Who knew where the bus would take me? Miles and miles from Dublin, for all I knew. And with everything falling apart, would Dad ever be able to find me? "I'm sixteen," I lied, straightening my back. "I can stay on my own. Please, get my mother from the bus and give her back to me. I won't let her out again, I promise." I was better off at Gran and Granddad's house, since it wasn't far from where they were taking Mom. I knew they wouldn't let anyone go to the medical bases to visit yet, but maybe eventually, and the RDS was close enough that I could ride my bike there.

The soldier shook his head at me. It was hard to tell with the mask on, but he seemed pretty young, in his twenties maybe. "She's out cold. You're better off without her for now. She'd only run again when she had the chance."

"She doesn't even have any ID on her. No one will know who she is." I patted my pockets, searching frantically for a pen and paper. "Her name's Noleen Seiler," I said, quoting my grandparents' address. "Will you write that down so the doctors know who she is?"

"Are you sure you're sixteen?" he asked, glancing down at my bare feet. "I think you should get on that bus."

A clamor from beyond the bus stole his attention. A group of ten to fifteen people with squared shoulders and surly faces advanced on the bus, one of them screaming the word "Fascists" over and over again. I made a run for it before the soldier had time to drag me onto one of the orphan buses.

I never turned to look back, but the soldiers must have

had their hands full with the rampaging ADS-infected because no one followed me. Back on Birchwood Street, where I finally slowed down, it was just me and the bearded man with the phone book again. He looked up from the Yellow Pages and smiled at me. "Don't be sad, love," he said. "The sun's still shining. Even if you haven't any ..." He paused as he patted the ground. I eyed my smudgy feet and realized he was trying to come up with the word *shoes*. My eyes were burning, but they hadn't spilled over yet. Even though the man wasn't all there, I guess he could see that I was on the verge of tears.

Now that he was smiling he didn't look like the type to bite, and I sniffled as I asked, "Why do you want to be out here? Why didn't you stay at home? And why are you reading the telephone book?" I didn't understand it. Why couldn't the sick people just stay put? Why did they want to run away all the time? Or maybe they didn't. Not all of them. Maybe there were thousands of ADS-infected still in their homes, curled up in their beds.

The man shrugged. "I don't try to tell you what to do now, do I? So why should you tell me?" He sounded so matter-of-fact about it that for a moment I felt like the messed-up one. I opened my mouth to argue with him because he *had* told me what to do — he'd told me not to be sad.

But there was no point in debating with someone who couldn't remember his own name. I clamped my lips shut as I peered down at him.

"You look like a fat lisp," the man said, mimicking me by puffing out his cheeks and making fishy lips at me.

A fat lisp? I was so tired of people who didn't make sense.

"I'm going home," I told the man as I shuffled by him.

The man saluted me. "Until tomorrow, love."

Alone, my feet felt chilly on the sidewalk and my arm smarted where I'd scraped the skin from it minutes earlier. With Mom gone I didn't know what to do. I thought of her unconscious on the bus, surrounded by other sick people, and a tear squeezed out of my left eye and slid down my face.

I walked zombie-like in the direction of Sykes Close, the air clammy around me. The place used to feel like a second home to me, but now everything just felt like sickness. I was so scared that the fear seemed like an illness of its own. Turning onto Sykes Close, I closed my eyes for a good ten seconds, hoping against hope that when I opened them again I'd be back in my bedroom at Gran and Granddad's that very first morning. No one would be shouting or walking around in a fur coat in summer weather. It'd be a normal July day in a month of normal July days in a normal country full of normal people.

I fluttered my eyelashes open and stared down my grandparents' street, at the front doors left gaping and the forsaken purple slippers in the middle of the road. Shuffling along the sidewalk I spied what had tripped me up earlier and allowed Mom to get away — a teaspoon. I picked it up and hurled it angrily at the nearest window.

The spoon clanked daintily off a front windowpane without causing the slightest damage. No one came to the door to see what the noise was. Either no one was home or no one cared. I felt like the last normal person left in Ireland.

Just then I caught a blur of motion from the corner of my eye, something dark and fast. Too quick to be a person. I swung my head to the right and stared hard at the space near the end of Deirdre Redmond's driveway. That's where the dim blur had been, only there was nothing to see, so it must have been a trick of the light. That and the shock of losing Mom.

I shivered, suddenly sure that I couldn't go back to Gran and Granddad's house, where every shadow and creak would make me jump. Feeling like the last uninfected person left in the country wasn't the same as being one. I wasn't even the last uninfected person left on the street. Ciara and Shehan were both within reach.

Shehan's place was nearest, and I began tromping up the driveway to his house, swallowing back tears and swiping my palm across my cheeks. I kept pressing his doorbell — *ding-dong ding-dong ding-dong ding-dong* — until the door swung open and Mr. Ranaweera emerged stiffly from behind it. Silently, he bowed and motioned for me to come inside like an old-time butler. "Where's Shehan?" I said, bounding into the hall with him.

My voice was a screech, and Mr. Ranaweera winced at the sound of it. Normally I'd have been more polite and waited for him to say something, but I knew he probably wouldn't, and even if he had, it wouldn't have been anything that could help me. He was at least halfway lost to ADS already.

I was opening my mouth to shout for Shehan when he careened downstairs with sleep still in his eyes and the hair on one side of his head matted. "My mom's gone,"

I croaked, before Shehan could get a word out. "She wandered off, and the soldiers took her."

Mr. Ranaweera's face was as emotionless as a starched hospital sheet as I ran through the details, feeling breathless and nauseated. Shehan put a hand on his father's back and said, "Dad, go sit down again, okay? I'll bring you some tea in a bit."

Mr. Ranaweera obeyed and disappeared down the hall, leaving Shehan and I alone. Shehan hunched over, stared at me with solemn green-brown eyes, and said, "You should stay here. Ring your dad and tell him you're here with me and my father." We both turned to stare at the last space Mr. Ranaweera had occupied. "He's not good," Shehan added, lowering his voice. "But I don't know exactly how bad he's got it because he'll hardly speak to me."

"At least he's still here." My tone was flat, but I meant to sound hopeful, and Shehan nodded.

"I've been trying to watch him. He was awake most of the night, listening to classical music on the radio. Just sitting there like a stone." Shehan clamped his lips shut, like he was stifling a yawn. "I must've drifted off for a bit earlier. It's a good thing you showed up when you did. Who knows what could've happened? I might have been out for ages."

"I was awake when my mom left." I stared down at what was left of the sparkly polish Ciara had painted onto my nails earlier in the week. "I couldn't make her stay."

Shehan didn't tell me everything was going to be all right or that we'd get my mother back somehow. I guess he knew better than to think he could make me believe that. "You did everything you could," he said.

"How do you know?" Maybe there was something else I could've said to her.

Shehan brushed his fingers against my arm. "I know you. It's how you are. And I know I can't tell you not to worry, but at least your mom isn't lost out in the street. Once they have a cure she'll be one of the first to get it."

I nodded, and a tear slipped down the side of my nose when I least expected it. "I'm going to get my phone from my grandparents' house." I batted at the wet streak with one of my sleeves, acting like it was more irritating than anything.

"Maybe some clothes too," Shehan suggested, glancing down at my bare feet like he didn't want to see me cry.

"Right. And then maybe we should get ahold of Ciara. See how they're all doing over there." Last I'd heard Ciara's parents were fine, which meant maybe I should've gone to her house instead, but now that I'd been to Shehan's I didn't want to leave him alone with his dad. I could help him watch his father, make sure Mr. Ranaweera didn't end up on a bus with a bunch of strangers and no one to look after him properly.

"Ciara's dad has it." The way Shehan said that made it seem almost inevitable. "I was talking to her earlier. She's not sure, but it seems like her mother might have the cough."

Which was exactly the way it started. I thought back to science class. Mr. Nishiada had told us measles was one of the most contagious diseases there was, that it could infect people through breath or touch almost instantly. He said ninety percent of people exposed to measles would catch it without the vaccines we have now.

"I hope her mother doesn't have it," I mumbled. I should've known Shehan and Ciara would be in touch. The last time I'd seen them together it'd been obvious they liked each other a lot more than I'd remembered. But Ciara and Shehan were the two people I had left. I didn't have it in me to be jealous the way I might've during a normal summer. "I should go get my stuff," I added, stepping back towards the door.

"Be careful," Shehan said.

And with that I edged through the front door and ran the rest of the way home.

NINE

THE LANDLINE WAS ringing when I darted into the house. Like so many other people on the street, I'd left the front door wide open when I'd left. My only thought had been catching up with Mom. Now I shut and locked the door behind me before racing into the kitchen and making a beeline for the cordless phone. Dad was on the other end of the line, and hearing his voice made me lose mine for a couple of seconds. All my hope was with him. He was somewhere that ADS hadn't touched — a place where people were still going to the beach, getting streaks in their hair, hitting softballs, and having picnics with tortilla chips and fruit salad.

Dad went quiet when I told him about Mom being sedated by the soldiers and carried onto the bus. I explained that I was going to stay at Shehan's, adding, "His dad's not well, but Shehan's fine and so is Ciara."

My father cleared his throat. "Don't let each other out of your sight. Stick with your friends. You'll have to call me on Shehan's landline from now on. When I couldn't get through to your cell I looked up the latest news on Ireland. The cellphone service there is overloaded, and the Internet's down."

It shouldn't have surprised me that cellphone service and the Internet weren't working, but it did. Every few minutes life took a turn for the worse. Normalcy fading.

"You do whatever you have to, Naomi," Dad said in a voice like a steel plank. "You hear me? Do whatever you can to stay well and safe. You and your friends need to keep a low profile. It might be difficult to tell who you can trust." It was hard enough listening to my dad be brave, but harder still when he added, "I love you. I'd do anything to be there with you right now."

"I know." I slapped away a tear with such conviction that one of my nails scratched my cheek. "I love you too. I'll talk to you in a couple of hours."

I hung up and jogged upstairs, like I had to do everything on fast-forward or the house would self-destruct. My suitcase was up in my bedroom, lots of the clothes I'd brought with me from Kingston still squished inside. Some of my other things were in the laundry room from when Mom had done a couple of loads on Thursday night, before she'd forgotten everything. Her clothes were mixed in with mine in the basket, and I fished out my stuff, crammed everything into my suitcase, and shoved my cellphone and charger inside one of the compartments too, in case service resumed.

I gathered up Mom's cheat sheet of info and the list I'd written for her, folded both in two, and slid them into my notebook. There was nothing to remind Mom of me now; I had to remember for both of us. My fingers shook around the pen as I dashed off another list.

BEST SEILER FAMILY MEMORIES

- The times (lots of them) when Mom, Dad, and I go bike riding together, and then for smoothies. If there's an especially nice sunset, Mom will make us all stop riding and watch.
- Making candy apples with my aunt, my cousin, and my dad back home about three years ago. My best apple was blue with coconut flakes. We were all laughing so much the whole time — even my dad and aunt — that I couldn't breathe.
- When Mom's friend Julia got married and Mom and I danced to "Happy" by Pharrell Williams, hips shaking and our feet kicking out in front of us, faster and faster.
- Eating chicken soup with my dad at our old house in Kingston when I was nine. It was so cold and snowy outside that school was canceled. We watched *Star Wars* movies all day.
- Seeing my gran and granddad at the airport when they come to pick us up every summer. They always look so happy.

There were so many more memories I could include, but I needed to go. I shoved my notebook into my suitcase along with everything else. Then I walked out of the house, locking the front door and pulling my wheeled suitcase quickly behind me.

At Shehan's door he answered himself this time, his hair spiky again and the sleep gone from his eyes. He looked relieved to see me. "Did you talk to your dad?"

I repeated what my father had said about cellphone

service as I stepped into the house. Shehan nodded like he already knew and then carried my suitcase up to his sister's bedroom. Mr. Ranaweera was sitting in the sunroom with a cup of tea, staring out at the backyard. We watched him from the kitchen while we talked. Shehan told me he'd called Ciara while I was gone and explained that I was going to stay with him. "Ciara would rather we all be together, but she said there's no way she could convince her parents to come over here. She's having enough trouble with them there, but at least her mum still finds their house familiar."

"And her dad?" I asked.

Shehan shook his head. "I don't think he knows much of anything at this point. They haven't been able to get ahold of her grandmother since she went to look in on a neighbor yesterday, either." So maybe her grandmother had gotten sick since they'd gone to see her last. More bad news.

Shehan explained that he'd been listening to lots of community radio from across Ireland over the past few days. According to what he'd heard, people had nicknamed ADS the "blackout flu" because in the same way blackout curtains blocked out the sun, ADS blocked people's memories, making them feel like strangers in a strange land.

"They say lots of them have been traveling in packs. Who knows where they think they're going. The theory is that the virus affects people differently. It sounds like most of the infected fall into roughly three categories: the blank, the blissed, and the bad."

"The bad," I repeated. "Are they the ones who are mad all the time?"

"Exactly. The troublemakers." Shehan folded his arms in front of him. "The blank are the ones that barely react, and the blissed are at total peace with everything even though they don't remember their own names." Like the woman who'd been serenely planting cutlery in her front garden. "But there don't seem to be as many of those. There are more of the angry or blank ones."

"My mom didn't really seem to be any of those." Definitely not blissed or blank. More like a stubborn kid who didn't want to be told what to do.

"Maybe the infection —" Shehan stopped and cleared his throat like he wanted to swallow back his words.

"Maybe the infection *what*?" I prompted.

"Maybe it wasn't full-force yet," he said apologetically.

My shoulders drooped. Maybe my mom had been in the process of turning angry and would become like the man who'd tried to start a fight with Mr. Kavanagh.

"But they said most people with the infection fall into those categories," Shehan reminded me. "That must mean there are exceptions."

I nodded slowly. "It feels like a nightmare. I mean, *mass amnesia*. Isn't that enough to worry about without people getting rabidly pissed off too?"

Shehan laughed lightly, shrugging with his elbows. "Could be worse, they could be vampires, hungry for our blood."

That wasn't very funny to me. We didn't know how much worse this would get.

"Sorry," Shehan said quickly. "I've been cooped up alone with my dad too long. I'm going a bit loopy."

"Yeah, me too. I keep quizzing myself to see if I have it. ADS, or blackout flu, whatever you want to call it."

"We don't have it."

"We can't be sure," I said.

Shehan's gaze skipped over to the counter across from us. There, sandwiched between two stainless steel kitchen jars, I spotted a purple envelope. The angle I was standing at allowed me to read the name printed across the front. *Naomi.*

"It's a gut feeling," Shehan said. "In a way it'd be easier to have it, wouldn't it? And so we won't get it because this is the harder thing, having to watch other people get sick."

That was a messed-up kind of thinking, but I knew what he meant. "I don't want to get it," I blurted out. "I just want everything back how it was." I strode across the kitchen and snatched up the purple envelope, my brain desperate for another distraction. "What is this?"

Shehan's voice dropped. "For, you know, your birthday."

Today. July tenth.

Today was my birthday. Today I was thirteen years old. I hadn't thought of that once all day. *I'd forgotten.*

My face fell. I swore under my breath, and Shehan said, "I wasn't going to say anything. It didn't seem right with your mum getting taken."

"You don't get it." The envelope felt cool against my fingertips. "*I forgot.*"

Shehan shook his head emphatically. "You forgot because it's one of the worst days of your life, not because you have it."

Maybe. Maybe not. I started mentally racing through state capitals to test myself. *Montgomery, Alabama. Juneau, Alaska. Phoenix, Arizona. Sacramento, California. Denver, Colorado. Hartford, Connecticut.*

No, wait. I'd already missed one. *Little Rock, Arkansas.* But then, it wasn't like I could name them off flawlessly before, either.

"You're not even coughing," Shehan pointed out. "You're grand. You're just shaken up, Naomi. Trust me. It doesn't mean anything that you forgot, and the last thing you probably feel like doing now is looking at this bloody thing." He stepped forward to take the envelope from my hand, but I didn't let go. "Okay, then. Open it if you want."

Shehan ran a hand through his shock of blue hair and stepped back again, leaning against the counter opposite me like he didn't know what I wanted.

"I'm sorry," I told him, ripping the envelope open and reading the greeting card. It was sarcastically funny and probably would've made me laugh if things had been different. Inside the card there was a gift card that said "One4all." I picked it up to stare at it more closely. "Thanks."

Shehan tapped his foot restlessly on the tile floor. "It's not like you can spend it now, but they take those gift cards at loads of stores here. Or they did. Before it went to hell."

"Thanks," I repeated, spontaneously closing the large gap between us and flinging my arms around him. I'd never hugged Shehan before. I'd never really hugged any guy my age, and I wasn't sure why I was doing it now, but it wasn't because of the gift card.

Shehan didn't exactly hug me back. Just sort of touched my back and a bit of my hair. Even that felt funny, like we were doing something wrong … but not wrong. Something that would have made my dad wish I were eleven or twelve instead of thirteen. Something that made me wish Shehan and Ciara were still only friends.

I let go of Shehan slowly, as though there was nothing strange about hugging him. The shadows outside were growing tall, and the natural light in the kitchen was beginning to dim. It didn't get dark in Ireland until about ten o'clock in July.

I glanced out at Mr. Ranaweera again. He looked like he was in a trance. He was one of the blank, for sure, and I told Shehan I was going to help watch over his dad and that we could take turns sleeping. I didn't think I'd be able to sleep a wink anyway. I was a messy combination of wired and sad that I couldn't shut off.

Shehan brought his dad into the living room, and the three of us sat in front of the TV watching the news. Every day the reporters and anchors were younger and there were fewer experts for them to interview but more anarchy in the streets. Nothing was open for business anymore, but stores were being looted by both ADS sufferers and those who weren't sick. Groups like the one I'd seen confronting the soldiers on Haverhill Road had been involved in skirmishes against military personnel and the police. The army numbers were dwindling due to illness, and reservists and other volunteers were struggling to keep the peace and maintain essential services. Riots were breaking out in the streets.

Fires continued to rage across the country because there weren't enough emergency service personnel to put them out. A young Dublin woman had given birth on the Ha'penny Bridge while trying to walk to the Rotunda Hospital for help with her labor. Luckily a teenage couple had happened upon her at the scene and helped deliver the baby.

In the middle of the news report the TV went dead and the living room floor lamp along with it. Shehan jumped up to get a flashlight and candles from the kitchen. We didn't entirely need them yet, but very soon it would be night.

First cellphones and then the electricity. That gave me a bad feeling, and judging by the look in Shehan's eyes, he had the same feeling. Mr. Ranaweera stared quizzically at the two of us in the dying light.

"Are you thirsty, Dad?" Shehan asked. "Hungry? Do you need me to get you something? We'll light the candles in a few minutes, okay? No point wasting them when we can still see."

Mr. Ranaweera didn't wait for the candles to be lit. He stood, casting a final look at us before he exited the room. Shehan followed quietly, me several steps behind him. We trailed Mr. Ranaweera upstairs, where he walked into the master bedroom and sat awkwardly on the edge of the bed, like he wasn't sure he belonged there.

I hung back and listened to Shehan say, "Why don't you lie down and get some sleep, Dad? I'll check on you later."

Shehan closed the door to his father's room and joined me on the stairs. "I don't know if he'll actually sleep or what," he said, breaking into a yawn himself. "I can't read him anymore."

"You should sleep," I told him. "I'll stay awake and watch over things."

Shehan shoved his hands down into his pockets and poked the inside of his cheek with his tongue. "I want to see if the power comes back. I wonder if the landline's still operating." Any cordless phones needed electricity to work, but Shehan and I hurried to the bottom of the steps where he picked up the slim corded phone that sat on an oval wooden table. His face was whiter than usual when he set it down again.

"No?" The word crashed out of my mouth.

Shehan shook his head, and I edged past him and pushed out the door, racing to Gran and Granddad's house. Maybe it was just Shehan's phone. Maybe ours would still work.

It had to. The telephone was the last thing left connecting me with family. I tore in the direction of Gran and Granddad's house, no other thought in my head. But as I neared their door my skin went cold. The same blur I'd glimpsed earlier swept along to the left of me, like something gliding through the air at ground level. A high-pitched mechanical-sounding chirp assaulted my ears. It came and went with a speed that made me wonder whether it had happened in the first place.

No bird alive sounded like that. No machine either. It was like nails on a chalkboard or the screech of a train as it whizzed into the station … and at the same time, not like that at all. Not like anything I'd ever heard.

Except ... except that very first night in Dublin. With everything else that had happened, I'd nearly forgotten about the ruckus that had erupted right before Mrs. Redmond had run out into the street.

My eyes didn't want to see what could make such a sound, but I forced myself to look, and just as I swung my neck to the right, Shehan called for me. Funnily enough, it was that regular sound that made me jump.

Shehan caught up to me in no time, and then his mouth was falling open and he was saying, "Who *was* that?"

"You saw it too?"

"It?" he echoed. "I saw something. I don't know who it was. It almost looked like ..." His fingers pushed roughly through his hair, the rest of his sentence paused in his throat.

"Like what?" I prompted, holding my breath.

"I can't describe it." Shehan's eyes scanned the empty air where the gliding figure had been. "Like someone in a wetsuit, maybe. Someone tall." Shehan pressed his eyelids together in concentration. "Wearing a helmet, maybe. I don't know. As soon as I saw them, they were gone."

"But the sound — that couldn't have been a person." Suddenly it occurred to me how stupid we were being, standing vulnerable in the middle of the road when whoever or whatever it was could've still been lurking nearby. I fished my key out my pocket and thrust it into the door, Shehan charging into my gran and granddad's house behind me.

I slammed the door shut behind us, the two of us gasping for breath. Our phone was lifeless like Shehan's had been, and for a full thirty seconds neither of us said anything.

Then Shehan murmured, "It had to be a person. Someone with ADS. Who knows what kind of bizarre sounds the infected can make? The virus is brand new. We barely know anything about it."

My gut told me he was wrong, but it was the only theory that made sense. The thing hadn't moved like a person, but then, I hadn't really seen it. "How much of a look did you get?" I asked.

"Not full on. Just out of the corner of my eye, really."

"Me too." I stalked into the living room and pulled back the curtain to survey the street. It looked just as we'd left it: absolutely empty. "It knows we're here," I said. "It saw us." I told Shehan that I'd seen it earlier too. "Maybe it's been watching us."

"You keep saying *it*," Shehan pointed out. "But *it's* a person. Probably a really sick person who doesn't understand what they're seeing or what they're doing."

We stayed in the living room discussing the possibility of whether it/they wanted to hurt us for so long that we lost every bit of remaining daylight. The moon must've been hiding behind a group of clouds, and with the power out Shehan and I could barely see in front of our own noses. "We have to get back," Shehan said finally. "We've left my dad too long already."

Anxious as I was, I couldn't argue with him; I wouldn't have left my mom alone overnight either. "We should come back tomorrow," I suggested. "Pick up supplies when it's light." It would be good to have everything in one place. And even with the thing around, it seemed important to stay near my gran and granddad's house. Besides, it may not have been any safer anywhere else.

"We will," Shehan agreed, the two of us pretending to be brave because there wasn't any choice. "Look, you give me the key and I'll lock up. That way you'll have a head start. I left my door unlocked."

"No way. We go together." Bad things happened when people stayed behind. I'd seen enough movies to have that idea stuck in my head.

"Okay." Shehan managed a crooked smile. "Together then." We stepped back outside, our eyes darting down the street for any sign of the blur. The way looked clear, and I spun to lock the door, Shehan keeping watch over the road. Then we full-out ran for his house like Olympic track athletes.

Less than a minute later we were safely back inside, Shehan heading upstairs to check on his dad while I prowled around on the ground floor with a candle, making sure no one had gotten in while we'd been gone. Nothing seemed out of place, and I didn't feel anything watching me from the shadowy rooms. For the moment, at least, we were alone.

TEN

I FILLED IN more pages of my notebook while Shehan was gone. After he joined me and confirmed his dad was fast asleep we brought the radio out to the bottom of the stairs where we could make sure Mr. Ranaweera wouldn't disappear on us. Neither of us said anything about the blur; we just sat there listening to the radio by candle-light. We kept running through stations — most of them community ones where regular people were giving their opinions about the crisis and spreading rumors that might have been fact. Some of them said that what was left of the government was in seclusion somewhere remote in the countryside. Maybe Donegal or even the Aran Islands. One man said that his brother-in-law worked for a cabinet minister and that some of the government had tried to take refuge on the Aran Islands because initially it'd been free from infection, but then the islanders had started taking sick with ADS too.

The one thing everyone seemed to agree on was that no one young had it yet. We switched over to RTE radio for a more official view of things. As usual, the news was bad. Without enough people to man power plants, it was unknown how long the electricity supply would be disrupted. "Clearly, we desperately require international intervention at this stage," a female broadcasting student from University College Dublin said. "But with the current lack of cure or treatment for ADS, so far the international community has been reluctant to send any of their own medical experts or military personnel. However, the British government has given indications that they are planning to airdrop aid supplies into Ireland if the situation continues to spiral downward."

"That's all well and good, but what's acutely needed is a peacekeeping force," a young male broadcaster commented. "Between the ADS mobs and the sudden rise of street gangs, we sorely need help in the area of security."

Almost everything I heard increased my panic. My brain was about to ignite. "Do you mind if we just switch it off for bit?" I asked.

"Good idea," Shehan said. "I know what else we can do."

Shehan nipped into the living room and came back with a box in his hands, taking the lid off to reveal a checkerboard. We'd played a couple of times years ago, and I'd usually lost. True to form, Shehan beat me twice in a row as the candle shrank. I thought I might have a chance at winning the third game, but when I captured one of Shehan's red checkers I noticed his eyes were closed.

He woke up with a start, stretching his eyes open wide as he fought sleep. "I think I'll bring a pillow and duvet down and just sleep right at the bottom of the stairs," he said. "You can kip in Sara's bedroom."

I pictured myself climbing the steps up to Sara's

bedroom, crawling under her covers, and lying awake every minute of the night, listening to the house groan and going insane with worry.

"I'm staying down here too," I offered. "I can settle down a little closer to the door. It'd be doubly hard for your dad to get by both of us." So far it seemed that Mr. Ranaweera didn't even want to run off like some of the others, but we had to be prepared. I wasn't going to let Shehan lose his dad the way I'd lost my mother.

We each brought a pillow and duvet down and lay on the floor like we were on an indoor camping trip. I wasn't sure if Shehan was still awake when I whispered, "The last time I was at a sleepover my friend's mother came down and yelled at us for talking too loudly in the middle of the night." That had been Lily's mother. She'd whipped into the family room where Alexis, Lily, Taneisha, and I had been stretched out on the carpet in sleeping bags. Then she'd screamed at a volume you could tell she regretted right after she'd done it.

"I bet you wish you were back at that moment instead of here," Shehan whispered back.

I couldn't see his face because I was lying on my side, turned towards the front door, but I could hear Shehan clearly. I folded an arm under my head on Sara's pillow and said, "Or in Kingston with my parents because they decided not to come back to Ireland this year." Glad as I was not to be alone, I missed my mom and dad so much that I had a constant pain under my ribs. Everything had changed in the blink of an eye.

"Jack's in Spain with his parents and his brothers,"

Shehan volunteered, referring to his best friend. "It's not that far, but it'd do me. If I could pick anywhere, I reckon I'd go with Australia, though. We were there once when I was eight. It was really laid-back and sunny and about as far from here as you can get."

"And your —" I was about to say his mom would be alive then too. My brain was sleepy and not quick enough in censoring my thoughts.

"What?" Shehan asked.

"Your mom," I said quietly, rolling back to face him. "I was just thinking she would've been in Australia with you then." Shehan didn't talk about his mother much, and I started to apologize for bringing her up.

"It's okay." Shehan's eyes were darker than the rest of him in the almost-blackness. "She was a laugh. You would've liked her. She liked to kick a ball around too. And she hardly ever raised her voice, even when she was angry. Not like your friend's mum. She was really ..." He searched for the right word. "Patient."

Shehan was right, I would've liked her. "I wish I could've met her." It wasn't fair that he'd lost her when she was so young.

"Me too," Shehan said thoughtfully. "Maybe there's some alternate universe out there where she's still alive."

"And where none of this ever happened." Because the virus wasn't fair either. It was stealing everything and everyone we know.

"Too bad we couldn't be *there*." Shehan's voice was light.

I didn't want to go to sleep feeling bad, and I don't think

he did either. We both started joking around again, naming other places and times we'd rather be. First good ones and then nasty ones like Siberia in wintertime; on a raft on the Amazon river in South America without a map; the time I got food poisoning from a hamburger I ate at a hockey banquet and couldn't keep anything down for three days; the time five years ago Shehan broke his femur and had to have an operation where a steel pin was pushed through the bone.

In short, just about anywhere except where we were. The conversation never officially ended. Somehow, we just fell asleep talking in the dark, and for a while I guess it was like we really were somewhere else.

DAY TEN

I woke up in the morning to the sound of a knock at the door. Mr. Ranaweera, with bewildered eyes and quivering lips, was looming over Shehan and me. Something told me he'd been standing in that spot a long while, trying to make sense of where he was and who we were. Shehan and I swapped nervous looks, the rap growing more aggressive by the second until Mr. Ranaweera stepped clean over our bodies and turned the knob. I barely had a chance to move out of the way before he opened the door.

My stomach clenched, expecting the worst, but it was only Ciara on the doorstep. She looked sad and tired, and Mr. Ranaweera abruptly turned and loped away, back upstairs. Shehan and I wriggled free from our duvets, talking over each other as we asked Ciara what was wrong.

"With the phone dead I couldn't ring," she murmured,

her hair fanning out behind her as it caught a gust of wind. "Mum's going to try to make it to one of the treatment centers with my dad. She wants to go now, when she thinks she'll still be able to handle driving the car. She says there's no way I'd be able to manage looking after the both of them once the ADS took her over. She thinks Adam and I would be better off with all of you here."

"Of course you should come here," Shehan said quickly. "Where's your stuff?"

"We're going to bring it soon." Ciara's voice splintered on the word soon. "I just wanted to tell you first." I reached out to touch her shoulder in sympathy, knowing how hard it would be for Ciara to say goodbye to her parents. Having adults we knew around felt reassuring, even if they weren't really themselves anymore. Now there would only be Mr. Ranaweera.

Shehan and I stood in the doorway watching Ciara walk back to her house. She hadn't said anything about seeing the blur, and maybe there was no reason to tell her. Maybe it had gone. Wandered off somewhere else.

With Ciara gone, Shehan, Mr. Ranaweera, and I ate breakfast at the kitchen table. Soon the food in the fridge would start to spoil. We needed to eat as much of it as we could first, and we started with tall glasses of orange juice, yogurt, and peach jam slathered on bread. My mind kept hanging on different images, some of them real and some of them powered by my imagination: Mom on a medical cot surrounded by row after row of anonymous screaming patients; the angry infected out on Haverhill Road, ready to charge the soldiers in their gasmasks; the man on Birchwood Street with the telephone book, laughing at me; ADS spreading across the Atlantic Ocean; masses of the infected terrorizing Princess Street in Kingston and shambling around Battery Park and the waterfront.

I forced the pictures out of my head and made myself concentrate on something useful, like taking out my notebook to make a list of the supplies we could retrieve from Gran and Granddad's later.

SUPPLIES FROM THE HOUSE
- All the food Mom & I bought at the supermarket a few days ago
- Buckets or other containers
- Blankets & towels
- Clothes
- Soap & shampoo
- Candles
- Matches
- Flashlights
- Batteries
- Bleach
- Toothpaste
- Gran's fondue pot

A friend of Gran's had given her the fondue pot for my grandparents' fiftieth wedding anniversary a couple of years ago. I remembered Gran wondering aloud what she would ever do with it because she didn't much like fondue. Mom had told her the gift could come in handy if the power was out because you could stick a little candle underneath it and pretty soon the pot's contents would be heated.

"After Ciara and Adam come we can get the things we need from my grandparents' house," I said. "The Kavanaghs' house too. We should take an inventory and start rationing out what we have." Whether the power came back on or not. We needed to outlast the ADS virus.

Shehan added that if the power stayed out the water treatment plants might not be operating properly, so we decided to start to stock up on water then and there. We began ransacking the kitchen, living room, and sunroom for anything we could fill with water. I turned the bathtub tap on full blast until water was nearly lapping at the rim and then I covered the precious contents with overlapping plastic wrap from the kitchen. Obviously the water was still flowing freely, but I had no idea if it was being purified or not.

On my way back downstairs the doorbell rang. Knowing it must be Ciara, I broke into a dash. Shehan was heading for the door too, and he reached it first. I heard Ripley's collar jingle before I saw anyone. Then Ciara handed Shehan a duffel bag and she and Adam stepped inside behind Ripley. Ciara and her brother were loaded down with several bulky cloth bags and a backpack each. Ciara's left fist was also clasping Ripley's leash, and as she made her way into the hallway Ripley wrenched her forward, snarling. Off balance, Ciara stumbled and dropped the leash. Ripley tore towards the kitchen, barking frenziedly.

I was the first one in after her. Poor Mr. Ranaweera was backed up against the refrigerator, cowering. There was more emotion in his eyes than I'd seen there since I'd arrived yesterday. Pure terror. Ripley would never hurt a harmless person, but I guess he didn't know that anymore.

I snatched Ripley's leash and yanked her close to me.

"Shut up, Ripley!" Ciara shouted from behind me.

Even though I had the dog, Mr. Ranaweera bolted. I'd thought Mom was fast, but Mr. Ranaweera ran like a police suspect you see on real-life cop shows, barreling through the sunroom and out into the backyard. The Ranaweeras' house was surrounded by wooden fences well over six feet tall and a gate that locked, which Shehan now held the only key for. Shehan was hot on his father's heels. There was little chance Mr. Ranaweera would get away.

Ciara, her brother, and I followed them into the back-yard, Ripley straining to break away from me with every ounce of her strength. Ciara, who'd dropped all her things in the kitchen, took the leash from me and yelled at Ripley again. "Ripley, *stop*!" The anger in Ciara's voice could've sliced a finger clean off, and this time Ripley whimpered and quit fighting for her freedom.

Meanwhile, Mr. Ranaweera was tackling the fence, try-ing to pull himself up and over. Shehan jumped into the air and threw his arms around his father's chest. The two of them tumbled hard to the ground, Shehan landing on his back and Mr. Ranaweera's fall cushioned by his son's body.

My legs flew me towards them. "Are you all right?" I stood ready to block Mr. Ranaweera if he still wanted to run. Shehan winced and released his hold on his father. "I'm okay. Just got a good thump on the way down."

I watched Shehan wriggle free, his father shifting his

weight until he was sitting on the lawn with his legs
unfurled in front of him, suspiciously eyeing Ripley.

"You scared him half to death with the bloody dog!"
Shehan bellowed at Ciara as he staggered to his feet. "What
the hell were you thinking, bringing it here? Are you
stupid or what? Because of you, my dad almost got away."

Shehan didn't normally raise his voice just like Ripley
didn't normally growl or corner people. Everyone and
everything had been changed by ADS, even if they didn't
have it, and when I saw Ciara flinch, I erupted too. "It's
not her fault, Shehan! What do you expect her to do —
leave Ripley behind?"

"If it comes down to a dog or my dad, yeah, I expect
Ciara to leave the mutt behind," Shehan said, his eyes
blazing. "Look at it." Shehan pointed down at Ripley,
who had begun to growl low in the back of her throat.
"She's frigging rabid. No wonder he panicked."

"There's nothing wrong with *her*." Ciara glanced at
Mr. Ranaweera on the grass. "She senses he's sick."

"And you brought her here knowing that?" Shehan spit
out. "You think your eejit dog is more important than my
father?"

"I thought … I thought she was over it. She barked at
my dad in the beginning too, and then she stopped." The
color was draining from Ciara's face, bitterness seeping
into her features in its absence. "Forget it, okay? Adam
and I will just *go* if we're not wanted here."

None of us, except maybe Mr. Ranaweera, had been
looking at Adam, but now my eyes skipped over to him,
the same as Shehan's did. Adam was rocking anxiously

back and forth on his heels, his eyes as round and wide as hubcaps. His hands were pressed tightly together, turning the knuckles white.

"It's okay," I told him. "No one's going anywhere, Adam. We all have to stick together." I shifted my gaze to Shehan, knowing that he might blow up at me next. I couldn't blame him for being upset because of his dad, but I couldn't let Ciara go. "We can keep Ripley in the backyard or something, can't we? She comes from two tough breeds. She'd be fine out here."

Shehan was still fuming, breathing hard and glancing from me to Ciara to Adam. I didn't know what I'd do if he said they couldn't stay. I didn't want to choose between my friends.

A voice from the lawn snapped our attention towards it. Mr. Ranaweera was saying, "This isn't right. I need *help*, Shehan." He looked like the genuine Mr. Ranaweera again, like he'd managed to climb back inside his own brain. He also looked even more afraid than he had in the kitchen. Not of Ripley, this time, but of what was happening to him.

"Dad." Shehan crouched down next to him, his tone pleading. "What do you want me to do?"

"I need to go … somewhere. I can't stay here like this." It was strange the way clarity changed someone's eyes. The life force in Mr. Ranaweera seemed a hundred times stronger than it had minutes earlier.

"They don't have a cure yet," Shehan said firmly. "We can take care of you until they do. It's chaos out there."

"The treatment centers," Mr. Ranaweera prompted, he

and Shehan rising to stand face to face with each other. "They said they were setting up treatment centers."

"They did. But we don't know what they're like." Shehan glanced apologetically my way. "They must be flooded with more people than they can take care —"

"We can't really take care of them either," Ciara interrupted. "Not when they get worse." Ripley's growl threatened to turn into a bark again. Ciara hunkered down on eye level with her. "I swear, Ripley, if you don't shut up I'm going to set you loose in the street and you can find your own dinner from now on."

Ripley looked away in regret, whining quietly.

"Maybe …" Ciara chewed her lip. "Maybe my parents haven't gone yet. They wanted me to come over here before they left. They could probably give him a lift to a treatment center if he wants one."

If looks could kill, Ciara would probably have fallen dead to the ground from Shehan's stare. Mr. Ranaweera answered for himself, "I want to go with them. It'll be easier for the four of you without me." Shehan began to argue with him, but Mr. Ranaweera raised his hand, silently asking Shehan to stop. "It's still my decision as long as I can think, Shehan. And this is what I want."

Ciara's eyes were filling. "I'll go check the house and see if they're still there," she said, pulling Ripley along with her. "Adam, you stay here. I'll only be gone a second."

"We should go together," I said for the second time in two days. So we all followed Ciara down the street to where Mrs. Kavanagh stood next to her red sedan, fiddling with a map. Mr. Kavanagh was tucked into the passenger seat with his seatbelt fastened, jaw slack and pupils dull.

Ciara rushed over to her mom, burying her head in her mother's shoulder. Mrs. Kavanagh tenderly kissed her hair. "Don't try to talk us out of it, love. We have to go now, before it's impossible."

"It's not that," Ciara said, and I could hear tears in her voice. "I still wish you weren't going, but I know you're not going to change your mind. We're just wondering if you can bring Shehan's dad with you."

Mrs. Kavanagh cast an appraising gaze at Mr. Ranaweera. Seeing the two of them coherent and in control of themselves made me miss my mom so much that for a second I forgot to breathe.

Mr. Ranaweera nodded at her. "I don't know how much longer I'll be lucid, but we don't have far to go if we head for the RDS. I'll do whatever I can to help."

"Take the map." Mrs. Kavanagh stepped closer and thrust it at him. "I can't seem to read it properly anymore. It's all just ... lines. I've been to the RDS so many times I shouldn't even need a map, but ..."

"I can go with you," Shehan volunteered loudly. "I can give you all a lift there and then come straight back. It won't take two seconds."

Mrs. Kavanagh and Mr. Ranaweera shook their heads in tandem. "We'll manage," Mr. Ranaweera says. "You should stay and look after the girls and Adam."

Given the situation, I probably shouldn't have minded Mr. Ranaweera saying it like that — as though Ciara and I, who were almost as old as Shehan, needed babysitting just because we were girls. It didn't bug me as much as it would've before, but it still made my ears hot the way they got when some people said women's hockey wasn't really hockey.

I watched Shehan hug his father goodbye and Ciara kiss her mother's cheek. At the last minute, Adam rushed in for a bone-crunching squeeze from Mrs. Kavanagh. Then Mr. Ranaweera and Mrs. Kavanagh hugged me too. "Take anything you need from the house," Mrs. Kavanagh said. "In fact, you should probably go through any of the unlocked homes and take all the food and supplies that you can. I think most of the houses on the street are empty."

Ciara, Ripley, Shehan, Adam, and I stood side by side as the red sedan backed slowly out of the driveway and into the road. We were still standing there after the car disappeared out of sight and the only thing we could hear was the sound of each other's disappointment at being well and truly on our own.

ELEVEN

RIPLEY WAS THE only one relieved to be rid of Shehan's and Ciara's parents. She was back to her usual self the second they'd gone. The four of us with arms instead of paws pillaged everything we could from Ciara and Adam's house, hauling stuff back to Shehan's. The Kavanaghs had a lot of canned and dried food, juice, and toilet paper too, but the best things were a camping stove, two propane canisters that felt full, and a box of water purification tablets.

Then we hit my grandparents' house. I found the fondue pot in the back of a kitchen cupboard and hugged it to my chest like it was gold. Gran and Granddad had a crank radio of their own and a ton of candles, flashlights, batteries, containers we could fill with water, and extra sheets and towels. There were so many things to carry that we had to make multiple trips, and on my third visit to the house, I headed up to the attic. My grandparents only used it for storage, but I didn't want to miss anything useful.

The narrow stairs creaked as I climbed them. The air smelled musty even before I reached the top. A sneeze forced my eyes closed. When I opened them I saw a woman lying on an old twin mattress.

Her black hair was matted to her head in a way that made her look like death. But she was unmistakably the same gloomy woman I'd seen sitting by the curb days earlier. Although she wasn't old, her skin looked nearly as dry as bark. When she looked at me — her blue eyes bloodshot — my heart skipped a beat.

Then I realized she was saying something, or trying to, at least. He mouth was moving, but her words gurgled in the back of her throat. I stepped closer so that I could hear her. She obviously needed help.

The woman's voice was so low that I had to bend down with my ear by her mouth. "Get out of my house," she whispered angrily. "Get out of my house."

I began moving away from her, but I wasn't fast enough. One of the woman's hands lunged for my hair and clenched at my roots. Her iron grip burned. I kept pulling away, struggling to get free. The more I fought — my two hands attacking the one she'd welded to my head — the more my scalp seared, and all the while the woman kept babbling, "Get out of my house. Get out of my house."

One of her nails sliced into the top of my head, the sting instinctively forcing me to heave in the opposite direction with enough strength to pull her from the bed. The woman thudded to the floor, her grip releasing me as she landed.

"Get out," she hissed from below, her voice gaining strength. I ran for the stairs, the woman reaching for my ankles even as she continued to tell me to leave.

On all fours, she chased me, crawling towards the stairs. I hurtled down them, the woman tumbling after me, head over feet. I thought the fall might stop her, that she could've even broken something. But the drop only paused her for a few seconds. Then she was crawling behind me again, the same five words jerking out of her mouth like a broken record.

As I began sprinting down the next stairway, Adam screamed from the bottom. He, Shehan, and Ciara must have heard the commotion. The three of them stared up at me in alarm.

And still the woman kept coming, creeping along on hands and knees. She'd never be able to catch me or any of us like that, but the fact didn't stop my heart from pounding. As I neared the bottom of the stairs, Ciara pulled the front door open so that the four of us could make a run for it. When my feet touched the ground I thought we were home free.

Adam had gone quiet, and with my back turned I didn't see the woman plunge down the second stairway, only heard the creak of the banister where she must have grabbed for it. She landed between us with a thunk, her head whacking against the floor.

We scuttled for the open doorway, only risking another look at her once we were outside on the doorstep. The woman hadn't moved a muscle. She lay face down on the floor, her hair stuck to the back of her head in clumps. "I think she's out cold," Shehan whispered, venturing a step closer to her. "She's still breathing."

"Close the door," I told him, my hands trembling. "We're out of here."

Shehan gingerly shut the door, and the four of us hotfooted it back to his house. We made it without another sign of her, but I couldn't keep the sound of the woman's voice out of my head. She'd really believed my grandparents' house was hers, but she hadn't wanted to let me go. Only her weakness had allowed me to escape.

"She must've gotten in when I ran after my mother," I said. It was the only time the door had been left open and unlocked, and there'd been no signs of forced entry around the house. "She's probably been up there in the attic ever since." I shivered to think that the woman had been lying upstairs the last time I'd spoken to my dad on the phone and when Shehan and I had slipped inside after spotting the blur.

Ciara smoothed some antibiotic lotion on my scalp where the woman had cut it with her nail and then, shaken and quiet, we all set about arranging the supplies in Shehan's front room. The woman's presence had forced us to leave some things behind, but there was a whole corner shop's worth of items anyway — from laundry detergent to powdered milk to kitchen sponges to baked beans. We decided to keep the curtain shuts, both to hide our existence and so no one would be able to see our things and be tempted to steal them.

Neither Shehan nor I mentioned the shadow we'd seen in the street to Ciara and Adam. We'd agreed not to beforehand, unless there was a reason to. There were already enough things to be afraid of, and while Shehan probably felt the woman in my grandparents' attic proved the shadow was an ADS sufferer, I didn't know what to think. The infected woman inside my grandparents' house had acted savage, but she'd still moved like a person.

For a long, long time no one said more than we had to.

Everyone must've been thinking about the threat practically outside our doorstep. It was only when we'd finished piling things up in Shehan's house that the spell of silence was really broken. "I reckon you and Adam should take my dad's room, since it's the biggest," Shehan said, looking over at Ciara from our tower of goods. "Naomi can sleep in Sara's, and I'll stick with mine."

"You want us to share a room?" Ciara said, giving off the vibe of someone who'd been insulted.

"Well, yeah." Shehan straightened a container that jutted out at an odd angle. "We only have three bedrooms. The box room is my dad's office — there's barely room to stand in it, let alone lie down."

That was something we should've thought about before we'd moved everything over to Shehan's. Ciara's place had four bedrooms. After all the time we'd spent hauling things, I didn't think any of us wanted to have to move them again, especially considering what had happened earlier.

Ciara arched her eyebrows. "But we're not even the same gender."

"You're related," Shehan pointed out. "I'm sure you've had to share a room before."

Adam nodded vigorously. "Her feet stink."

"You're ridiculous, Adam." Ciara glared up at the ceiling, refusing to look at him. "Do you think anyone would believe that? When was the last time you even washed your feet? You're a walking dirt trap."

Between the livid woman at my grandparents' house and not knowing whether we'd ever see our parents again, there probably wasn't one of us who could think clearly —

we were all strung out on stress. But I couldn't believe that after everything we'd been through Ciara was still letting Adam get to her. I wished someone I was related to was still around.

"Grow up, Ciara," Shehan snapped.

Ciara's eyes caught fire. I felt her simmer next to me, her mind sifting through angry words to sling back at him. She and Shehan had barely gotten over this morning's fight and here we were again. It felt like they'd just been waiting for the chance to blow up at each other afresh.

Well, if that was the way this was going to go, I didn't want to hear it. "Everyone shut up!" I shouted, sick of the squabbling. We hadn't been together a day yet and we were already falling apart. How would this ever work if we couldn't pull together? "You're all driving me crazy. I'm going upstairs where it's quieter!" My own eyes glowered as I turned and walked off in a huff.

I was so mad that I grabbed my grandparents' crank radio and took it up to Sara's room with me. But then I was too angry to even listen to it. Before I knew it, my fingers were snatching up a pen and writing out another list to distract myself — pretending I was anywhere but here, like Shehan and I had talked about last night. The places I'd already been were easiest to picture in my head, but even though I was trying *not* to think about where I was, Dublin was the first place I wrote down.

PLACES I'VE BEEN
- Dublin, Ireland — every year. Right now I hate it! But before I probably would've written that it feels like a

second home and that when I get back to Kingston my ears miss the accents and everything people say sounds really F-L-A-T.

- Disney World, Florida — best parts are the Pirates of the Caribbean ride, the Haunted Mansion, and the Seven Dwarfs Mine Train. But I love everything — the daytime parade, closing fireworks, and even the Country Bear Jamboree, which is really meant for little kids.

- Ottawa — so cool to skate on the Rideau Canal. Since it's only a couple of hours away from Kingston I've been a few times. When you're gliding on ice you don't have to think about anything else. Your mind is clear.

- Toronto — close to Kingston too. I've been up the CN Tower and watched the Blue Jays play. Once I saw Tom Hiddleston (Loki) crossing the street. If Loki were here now he'd probably tie up everyone downstairs and gag them so they'd stop getting on his nerves.

- Montreal — pretty close also but feels so different from Toronto. A few years ago I told my dad that when I grow up I'm going to live in the Plateau where there are so many amazing shops and cafés. I still want to do it. I want to close my eyes, then open them and be standing on Avenue du Parc.

- Seattle — my dad's friend Naoki lives there, and we went to visit a few years ago. My dad loves the view of the mountains and says if he were a place he would be Seattle.

- Philadelphia — they have a kids' museum where you can touch everything. I was pretty young when I was there so I don't remember much else, but there's a photo of me and my mom in front of the Liberty Bell.

- Quebec City — went with the rest of my grade this past spring. A cute French guy in a school uniform winked at Alexis and me in the Couche-Tard (Quebec convenience store chain). Now I basically have my own Couche-Tard downstairs and everything's free, but who cares? Everything SUCKS.
- London, England — for three days when we had to fly there before connecting to a flight to Dublin. In the underground (subway) there they have the longest escalators I've ever seen. Also really amazing street musicians busking in the stations.
- Marbella, Spain — mostly spent at the beach. The Spanish people were so nice, like you already knew them well enough to have dinner at their house.

When my list was finished, I read it over three times, wondering if I'd stumble across it in future days or weeks and have no clue what I'd been talking about. Once Mom's ADS got bad she didn't care about the things she'd written down about herself. They meant nothing to her.

When it came down to it, it was impossible for me to quit thinking about the virus. I turned back towards the radio, rotating the hand crank to power it up. Dialing through the stations there was lots of dead air, but soon I stumbled across the BBC. A newscaster said, "Public Health England and the CDC have determined that while people in their very early twenties or younger show no symptoms of ADS, they still carry and transmit the highly contagious virus. It's believed the fact that young brains are still developing somehow protects them, preventing memory loss and the virus's other symptoms. Unfortunately, virtually everyone over the age of twenty-one or twenty-two who is exposed to ADS quickly develops memory loss."

That meant we all had ADS. Me, Shehan, Ciara, and even Adam. Each of us had been exposed. But none of us would get sick. We wouldn't forget. A flame of happiness sparked inside me.

"Research indicates that ADS's impact on the brain is closer to amnesia than to degenerative neurological conditions like Alzheimer's disease," the newscaster continued. "Memory loss and unusual behavior are the chief symptoms of ADS. But scientists now theorize that brain damage doesn't continue to progress in ADS sufferers, instead stabilizing after several days, whereas as dementia advances bodily functions are ultimately lost, eventually leading to death. While there remains only one known case of ADS in mainland Britain, British health officials are warning anyone suffering from flu-like symptoms or sudden memory loss to quarantine themselves and call Britain's ADS hotline."

Just one case still. They were lucky.

The whole world wouldn't catch this. There was hope. People with ADS wouldn't get any sicker than they already were. They wouldn't lose their ability to walk or talk or other things. They would live.

Unlike Gran. She would only get sicker with Alzheimer's. Sadness pierced my hope, sudden tears forming in my eyes. Mom had told me Gran's condition would slowly worsen, but I never knew just how bad it could get. Even if scientists could cure ADS, Gran would still be sick.

Somehow, I had to keep enough hope for all of us; I couldn't give up on anyone. Science learned new things all the time, didn't it? Maybe it could one day heal Gran's Alzheimer's too.

I ran my finger along the dial, listening for signals. RTE didn't have news people on all the time anymore — now there was a message repeated on a loop announcing their next broadcast would be at nine o'clock tomorrow morning — but I found a few of the community stations Shehan and I had listened to the day before. Some of the people on them had had violent run-ins with the ADS-infected, especially when they were in packs. Most of the army had disintegrated, and there seemed to be no one but people's neighbors and what was left of their families to help fight off the infected.

One woman said her father had tried to kill her with a golf club, and when she'd raised her arm to defend herself he'd slammed the club against it, breaking her arm. She'd only survived because her younger brother had tackled their father to the ground. Overall it sounded like I'd gotten off easy in suffering only a tender scalp. Not everyone's stories were scary, though; some of them were just sad, and one guy even said that a blissed woman had saved him from a group of others.

Hearing just how bad things were out there made me feel almost as bad as I had before I'd learned my friends and I wouldn't get sick. Fear had begun spreading inside me like a growing branch. I didn't want to be alone anymore, hiding away on an upper floor like the creepy woman in my grandparents' attic.

I hurried downstairs to tell everyone the things I'd heard, my eyes darting into the front room as I walked along the hall. The door was open, Shehan and Ciara alone inside. His arm was wrapped around Ciara's shoulders and he was saying something in a low voice into her ear. She nodded gingerly and rested her head against his shoulder. They looked so close in that moment, like the last thing they wanted was to be interrupted.

My heart sank as I spun on my heel. With the way Shehan and Ciara had been arguing today I'd wondered if I was wrong about them. No such luck. And it was one thing for Shehan and Ciara to like each other, but did they have to be so obvious about it right in front of me?

I needed to be somewhere else for a minute, even if that just meant the backyard. Ripley would warn me if anyone came near. Besides, Shehan's yard backed onto parkland and his fence was tall. Only Shehan's neighbors on either side would've been able to see into his yard from their upper floors. The dark-haired woman couldn't possibly spot us from my grandparents' house, and soon she wouldn't even remember us.

Ripley came running when I called for her, Adam tagging along behind. Together, the three of us trooped out into the yard.

"Are we safe out here?" Adam asked, eyes darting around.

"Safer back here than in the front. I don't think the woman will come after us if we don't go bothering her. She just seemed to want to be left alone." I hoped what I was saying was the truth. "Come on, let's throw Ripley a few."

We'd only been tossing the ball around for a couple of minutes when Ciara and Shehan scrambled outside with us. Neither of them said anything about my outburst. Ciara's tone was unusually nice as she suggested, "Maybe we should try to cook something on the stove. Before the food goes bad."

My stomach rumbled in agreement, and between the four of us we pulled pork chops, sirloin steaks, cauliflower, eggplant, spinach, and frozen french fries out of the dead refrigerator. Everything still felt cool, so maybe we'd be able to eat a couple of the other things left in there tomorrow. Then we carried the camping stove outside and set it on the patio. It was easy to use, but it took a while to cook everything since the stove only had two burners. On top of that, none of us had ever fried pork chops or steak, so we had to keep slicing into them to check their progress.

While we were eating and washing the food down with pint glasses of milk — all of us making an extra effort to get along — I explained what I'd heard on the BBC.

"So we must have it, then," Shehan said, sliding one of his palms against the side of his cheekbone, like he was looking to find a place it would fit.

"I don't feel any different, but, yeah, we must." ADS was just lying in wait.

"Does that mean we'll get sick when we get older?" Ciara asked.

All of us were silent for long seconds, her question forcing us to imagine years of this — no power, no safety, the street empty of adults except for those who might attack us.

"I'll be the last one who gets it, then," Adam said finally.

"If it lasts that long I'm swimming to Wales," Shehan joked, obviously trying to lighten the atmosphere. "There's no way I'm sticking around here without Internet and electricity and having peanut butter and baked beans for dinner for the next six years."

"We can build a raft," Adam enthused. "Like when people get shipwrecked in a movie."

Ciara popped a fry into her mouth. "You won't need to build one. Just steal one of the boats floating in Dun Laoghaire harbor."

"Right, and then we can all infect the nice people in Wales," I said dryly, pausing with my fork in the air. "Although, now that I think about it, maybe they're not all that nice. What have they done for us lately? Everyone's just leaving us here to rot."

"Good point." Shehan held up his glass like he was making a toast. "Screw Wales."

"Screw Wales," Ciara, Adam, and I echoed, holding up our glasses too.

I gulped down more milk, feeling it slosh around in my stomach along with everything I'd eaten. We'd each really stuffed ourselves. I felt a bit sick by the end of the meal, and Ciara looked green.

Ripley got the leftover steak along with her dog food, and then we washed the dishes in about two inches of water because we didn't want to waste any. Already we'd decided to scoop the water from Shehan's tub into one of the Rubbermaid containers so that we could still use the bath to get clean. No long showers or full baths for us anymore, though. We were rationing.

Later we played old board games by candlelight, everyone letting Adam win more times than he lost. Every so often I caught Shehan staring at me like I had a piece of spinach stuck between my teeth. Maybe he'd guessed I was mad at him for liking Ciara after all. I really hoped not; that would be so humiliating. And anyway, I couldn't make the anger stick properly. It was just too bad that I'd gone and grown new feelings for Shehan at the same time that he and Ciara had grown them for each other instead.

When we blew out the candles at eleven o'clock and climbed the stairs, it occurred to me that I could offer to share a bedroom with Ciara so that she wouldn't have to put up with Adam and he wouldn't have to put up with her. But I never opened my mouth to do it. While I wasn't exactly mad at my friends, the thought of them looking so cozy together earlier didn't leave me feeling generous either.

TWELVE

IN THE MIDDLE of the night, I woke up to the sound of low but agitated voices in the hall. I knew it was the dead of the night because I'd taken one of Gran's watches with me earlier and it'd been fastened around my wrist ever since. If you pressed one of the buttons at the side of it, the watch's face was bathed in green light.

I lay under Sara's covers listening to the rise and fall of the voices. One of them belonged to Ciara, and the other wasn't deep enough to be Shehan's so it must have been Adam's. A cough racked through one of their chests. *A cough?* The BBC had said young people couldn't get sick, but a cough was one of the main symptoms of ADS. The sound pushed me out of bed and into the hall.

It felt darker there than it had in Sara's room. I should've known better, but I reached for the light switch. Of course, nothing happened. I stepped back into the bedroom and reached for the flashlight on the nightstand. We'd each taken one to keep with us overnight. I clicked the flashlight on and advanced into the hall again, following the sound of the cough towards the bathroom. The door was closed, and I rapped softly.

Ciara opened it to reveal Adam bent over the toilet in

the stark shadows created by her own flashlight. Adam was puking his guts up, not coughing, and relief shot through me. "I think he ate too much at dinner," Ciara said.

We all did. *But wait.* Could it be the water? Maybe it wasn't being purified anymore. The puke smelled nasty, and Ciara reached over Adam's head to flush the toilet. "We brought all the pills from my house over here," she said to me. "I know we had something for motion sickness."

"I'll go down and find it," I volunteered. Poor Adam.

I aimed the beam my from my flashlight down the steps, trailing the glow to the bottom of the staircase. On the main floor I veered into the front room. We'd put all the medication together in a large shoebox, and I rooted around, trying to locate it. Two minutes later I had the medicine box in my hand. A chill ran down my back as I opened it.

Aside from the blur and the ADS woman in my grandparents' house, there hadn't been a sound from the outside world in days, but now male voices clattered in the street. Not boys' voices, but men's. I edged over to the window, tempted to inch the curtain open and glance out at them. On second thought, what would they do if they saw me? If they were the bad kind of infected they might try to get inside. It was safer not to look.

I shut off my flashlight and listened closely, struggling to make out their words. One of them sounded close. So near that I was almost afraid to move.

But if I didn't take the box up soon, Ciara was bound to come looking for me. That thought carried me back upstairs in total darkness. I didn't knock on the door before opening it this time. I swung it open, handed her the pills, and whispered, "There are some men outside. I heard them shouting to each other in the street."

Ciara's eyes widened. "Did you get a look at them? Are they infected?"

"I couldn't risk peeking. One of them sounded like he must be just at the bottom of the driveway."

Adam was sitting down by the toilet and staring at me as though I'd said I'd seen a ghost. Ciara set the pills down on the counter and told him to stay where he was. She left her flashlight in the bathroom with him as the two of us stepped into Sara's bedroom. Ciara froze when she got her first earful of the voices. They were loud and excited in a way that froze me too. If they were infected they wouldn't be as easy to evade as the woman had been. These ones sounded strong. Only when their din had faded did I pinch the curtain between my fingers and pull it back a sliver. I got a glimpse of the men's backs as they made their way hastily up the street and receded from view. "There are two of them," I whispered. "Both over six feet tall."

"How old?" Ciara asked.

As I opened my mouth to answer I spotted something else close to the front door of a house across the street. Something black, sleek, and long that was partially hidden by an overgrown bush. It could've been a clump of garbage bags the men had left behind, but the longer I looked at it the frostier I felt.

"What is it?" Ciara said.

"I ... I don't know. There's something out there.

Something that wasn't there before."

"What do you mean *something*?" Ciara's voice had turned nearly as urgent as the men's had been seconds earlier. She pushed in next to me at the windowsill, and I pointed out the lump of black.

We were both staring at it so fixedly that neither of us heard Adam enter the room. "What's going on?" he whispered from behind us. Ciara and I jumped, Adam pointing at the thing and asking, "Is that a body?"

"No," Ciara denied, too late.

"I'm getting Shehan!" Adam cried. The sight of whatever had been left out in the street seemed to have temporarily stopped him throwing up. He was already turning, running for Shehan's room.

Twenty seconds later Shehan was standing next to us too. The four of us huddled in front of the window as Ciara and I explained about the men.

"Did they see you?" Shehan asked.

I shook my head confidently. "We didn't glance out the window until they were going. That's why we didn't get a good look at them."

"And did they sound infected?"

Neither Ciara nor I could tell. "They were shouting a lot, but we couldn't make out what they were saying," I replied. Adam's hand flew to his mouth. He spun to run back to the bathroom, Ciara following him. With Shehan and I left alone I said, "What do you think — could it be the woman from before wrapped up in something?" A funeral shroud, maybe. But who would've done that for her, and why leave her out on the lawn?

"I reckon it could be anything. Someone's rubbish."

"Could be. But we should check." We had to know what we were dealing with.

"Tomorrow in the daylight," Shehan suggested.

We'd have more courage in the sun, for sure, and I nodded before explaining about Adam being sick and my hopes that it had only been from too much food, not because the water was bad. "It sounds like it's time to dig out those water tablets," Shehan said with a frown.

A sick boy. The possibility of bad water. All our parents gone while the ADS-infected and unknown intruders skulked around Sykes Close. Some mysterious thing that might have been a body lying across the street. Weren't we overdue for some good luck?

Back in Sara's bed I tossed and turned, half-expecting to hear men's voices outside again. When I couldn't take it anymore I reached for the radio, whirling the hand crank around until the power light came on. Inching the volume down, I listened to conspiracy theorists share their pet ideas — that ADS was a biological weapon being tested by a foreign country, that it was the work of highly organized terrorists, that it was sent by an angry god to punish people for being too materialistic.

Each of the theories sounded as crazy as the last to me, but then again, the ADS outbreak was the craziest thing I'd ever seen up close. A couple of people said they'd seen clusters of the infected heading for the coasts. "I reckon they might be trying to get off the island," a guy who sounded like a teenager said. "If they manage to do it, we could be in deep trouble. What's to stop the UK or any other country from flying over and blasting this place to kingdom come to keep their own countries free from blackout flu?"

Surely the United Nations wouldn't let that happen. Why would the infected want to escape Ireland when they couldn't even remember their own names? There were so many rumors and no way to be sure which, if any, were true.

If my parents had been here they'd have noticed how the things I heard on the radio were upsetting me and made me turn it off. But I didn't have the luxury of staying in the dark now. We needed to know what was going on out there.

DAY ELEVEN

I listened to people tell their stories and share their theories until the sun began to rise. Then I made my way downstairs in the glint of early morning light. Ripley, who didn't have to stay in the backyard because Mr. Rana-weera was gone, greeted me in the downstairs hall. As I stepped into the kitchen I noticed her water dish was dry. I searched out the water purification tablets, filled the milk container we'd polished off last night to the halfway point, and dropped in a tablet. *Use one tablet per one liter*, the instructions said, *and let the water sit for thirty minutes after the tablet has dissolved*.

I didn't need to keep writing my journal entries or lists anymore; it didn't sound as if I would come down with ADS anytime soon. But something inside me wanted to keep going. Taneisha's therapist was right — it helped. It made my mind leap forward into a future where ADS was behind us. So I sat at the table to jot down another list while the purification tablet worked its magic.

PLACES I HAVE NEVER BEEN & WANT TO GO WHEN THIS IS OVER

- Shanghai — because it looks like the future. The very first thing I would do is ride the magnetic levitation train from the international airport to the city; it can go more than 270 miles per hour.
- Egypt — to see the pyramids and Cairo and Siwa Oasis, which looks like a place from a dream.
- New York City — because when Taneisha came back from there she said it was the absolute best place she's ever been, like a light bulb somehow turned up extra bright.
- The International Space Station — to stare at Earth from the stars.
- Cedar Point, Ohio — they have sixteen roller coasters, and it's the only amusement park in the world with five roller coasters taller than 200 feet!

With the thirty minutes up, I shoved my paper aside to slosh the water into Ripley's dish. Shehan appeared in the kitchen in Nike jogging pants, a severely rumpled T-shirt, and bare feet. I looked down at them for a second too long, which made him look down too.

It's not like his feet were anything new to me. I was being an idiot — the queen of bad timing. If I was going to notice Shehan it should've been before he'd grown on

Ciara. Now was no time for things like that, anyway. We needed to stay focused on getting through this.

My gaze soared to his face. "I guess they didn't come back again last night."

"I guess not." Both Shehan's hands dug into his messy blue hair. "I hope Adam's feeling better today."

"Me too." I pointed to the purification tablets on the counter. "I put one of these in Ripley's water."

Shehan picked up the package and turned it over, reading the fine print. "They expired in April. Do you think they'll still work?" I hadn't even thought about an expiry date, and I felt my face fall.

"They must still do *some* good," Shehan said, his eyes on me and then Ripley. Near my feet she was lapping up the contents of her dish, at first energetically and then with less enthusiasm. "I don't think she's impressed," he added. "I've heard some of those tablets make the water taste like a medicine cabinet."

Great. "We can boil water, anyway, while we have propane. And I remember my science teacher saying you can add drops of bleach to make water drinkable if you can't boil it." I wondered if that would taste as unappetizing as the tablets. "Or we could leave containers outside to fill up with rainwater. That should be clean enough."

"It sounds like I should've paid more attention in science class." Shehan curved his toes under his feet. "We could set containers up today."

I thought of the unknown thing we'd seen last night and felt a stubborn courage well up inside me. I couldn't do anything about the things I'd heard on the radio during the night, but I could march across the street and see the thing with my own eyes — solve at least one mystery. "And go have a look at whatever we saw last night," I said. "Let's do it right now, get it over with before Ciara and Adam wake up."

I was usually the one who insisted we stick together, but what if it the thing across the street was something Adam shouldn't see or that would put him in danger? If Ciara was going with us he'd insist on coming too, and that would be another argument.

Shehan's eyes were uncertain. Maybe he didn't want to leave Ciara behind unprotected. Now that they'd stopped fighting and were back to being *close* it was natural that she was the person he'd worry about most, even if I didn't like to think about that.

"Why don't you stay here and set up the water containers," Shehan suggested. "I'll go look." His gaze hardened, like he could see my protest coming. "It won't take long. I'll be back in a tick."

"You're not going alone when we don't know what's out there," I countered.

"That's why I should go solo — because we *don't* know what's out there. We don't want a repeat of that woman in the attic, or worse." Shehan's fingers shot out to touch my elbow. "Not that I think there will be — I'm sure it's just a heap of rubbish, nothing to worry about — but I'd feel better if you stayed here."

"And I'd feel better if we went together," I said, determination tugging at my cheeks and jaw. His concern felt nice — nicer than it should've, considering he was Ciara's boyfriend — but mine was just as strong. "So our opinions cancel each other out. Which means I'm coming."

"Shouldn't canceling each other out mean neither of us goes?" Shehan suggested, amusement and irritation struggling against each other in his grin.

"Nope." I smiled back through gritted teeth. "Even if you want to blow up at me like you did with Ciara, I'm coming with you."

Shehan shook his head like I was driving him crazy; meanwhile, his grin hadn't quit widening. "You blew up too, remember? *Scary*. I wouldn't want you as an enemy."

"Ditto. Maybe we need to make a rule. No blowing up. I know it's just the tension from everything lately, but ..."

"No, you're right." Shehan bit his lip. "It doesn't help to get angry. We need to stay calm. Once we check out whatever's across the street and sort out clean water, everything will be fine."

Did he really believe that?

"Course it will," I agreed with more confidence than I felt. "There's plenty of food." As long as no one stole it. As long as we were careful about how much we ate. As long as Adam got well and no one else fell sick. The list went on and on inside my head.

"Anyway." One of my teeth scraped against the inside of my cheek. "Let's go do this, the two of us."

"Okay, then," Shehan conceded, his eyes almost as unsure as they'd been minutes earlier. He grabbed a piece of scrap paper and pencil from behind a flour jar on the counter and jotted down two sentences for Ciara and Adam.

We left the note at the foot of the stairs and crept

outside in the same clothes we'd slept in last night, Shehan locking the door behind us. The air felt cool, and a rain-drop grazed my cheek as we approached the thing across the street. In the daylight it was clearly body-shaped, curved in on itself like it'd been folded at the waist, and I slowed down, remembering how Shehan had described the blur. Like someone in a wetsuit.

Now that I could get a better look at it, I saw it wasn't a wetsuit exactly, but it seemed to be something similar. A bodysuit that covered every inch of the thing. The part where I guessed the head should be was still hidden by the bush, and I stopped entirely, my stomach bottoming out.

"It's too thin and tall to be a normal person," Shehan said, the two of us standing so close together that our shoulders were touching. He was right: a normal person wouldn't have been able to bend that way. Not alive, anyway. But it wasn't just that — the entire mass of the thing looked wrong.

I stared at the black second skin, watching for any sign of movement and resisting the urge to turn and run back to Shehan's house. "If it moves ..." I began.

"It if moves, we leg it," Shehan continued. We gripped each other's hand, walking up the driveway in step. Neither of us had thought to bring gloves, and Shehan was the first to reach down and touch the thing's leg. "It feels cold," he said.

I walked around the bush and stared at its head, which was twice the size of mine. There was no break in the black second skin covering it, so unless it could breathe through the fabric, it must've been face down. "We need to turn it over," I whispered — as though the thing could still hear us — fighting the temptation to flee.

But we had to see, didn't we? We couldn't walk away leaving it an unsolved puzzle.

Shehan hesitated. Our eyes locked over the body. "Okay," he said slowly. "Grab its shoulders."

I flinched as I crouched down near the thing. But Shehan had touched it. If he could, I could. I flung my right hand out and grasped what I estimated was the thing's shoulder. The bodysuit felt chilly like a stone. My left hand curved around the other shoulder, and together Shehan and I rolled the thing over on the lawn. The dark second skin around its head caught on a twig from the bush next to it. The protective covering ripped open with the speed of a rubber band snapping, and I recoiled, falling backwards. As the body flipped over, unsupported except for Shehan at its legs, the naked face of the thing pointed blankly up at the sky.

I choked on air at the sight of it. The skin was a gray so near to white that it made the figure look almost albino. The thing's face was as smooth as baby skin, like it had never been out in the sun. There were tiny holes on either side of its head, where you'd have expected ears to be, and its enormous, wide-set eyes seemed to have rolled back in their sockets because I couldn't see any pupils, just pools of white. The nostrils were barely more than slits, and the mouth was long and protruding, sort of like a gorilla's.

"Not human," Shehan rasped. "That thing was never human."

I nodded numbly, still trying to catch my breath. A

virus that stole people's memories was one thing, but I didn't believe a virus could have done *this*. Didn't want to believe it. If this was what became of the infected, we were all doomed.

THIRTEEN

I DIDN'T WANT to be near the thing anymore. Staring at it was making me feel nauseated. I could hardly believe it was real and not some Hollywood creation. Neither Shehan nor I wanted to touch the thing again, but seeing it lying there with its face exposed didn't seem right either. In the end Shehan hopped into the backyard to unlock the fence, and we dragged it back there and left it next to a garden shed. The body was surprisingly light considering how gangly it seemed.

Only once we'd closed the gate behind us and begun walking back to Shehan's house did our eyes really meet again. "Are you all right?" Shehan asked, a film of sweat spreading across his forehead.

How could I be?

"What was *that*?" I whispered, as though it still might be able to hear us. "The virus couldn't … couldn't mutate someone like that, could it? That wasn't a person, right?" He'd said so himself, but I needed to hear it again.

"I don't think so." Shehan's fingers rubbed his forehead. "Listen, this is going to sound completely mad, but a few days ago — before you came over to stay — I heard a couple of people on the radio say they saw something crash into the water near Dalkey."

"Crash? You mean, from the sky?" He hadn't said the A-word, but my mind was feverishly circling it. "Why didn't you tell me that before?"

Shehan shoved his hands into his armpits. "Because I thought they were loonies. Either that or they were already sick. But they said ..." Shehan blinked in double time. "They said the crash was a couple of days before the virus hit, and that a few hours afterwards a friend of theirs spied *things* coming out of the sea. They reckoned these things — these alien things — were what brought the virus."

I would've written them off as crazies too if I hadn't just seen the thing across the road with my own eyes. "On purpose?" I asked.

"Who knows?" Shehan said. "I only heard them the once, and I didn't listen for very long. I never thought they were talking sense."

It was hard enough to process the reality that I was stuck in a country ravaged by ADS, my mother possibly turning bad in a medical base bed alongside scores of others who were equally as sick, but the idea of extraterrestrials infecting people turned my blood to ice in my veins. I focused on Shehan's pupils, fighting the sensation that I was falling — a skydiver without a parachute.

"Maybe we should've just left it alone," I murmured. "Not moved it. Do you think it was keeping us under surveillance?"

"I don't know. If it was sick maybe it just couldn't leave the area. We don't know if the disease ..."

Killed it. Yet so far no humans had died from ADS.

I laced my hands together to stop them from trembling. "I heard some other wild things on the radio last night," I began. Now that we knew aliens were real, anything seemed possible. I told Shehan what the conspiracy theorists had said, and about the infected trying to get off the island.

"We better hope that's not true." Shehan shuddered. "If that happens the whole world could get infected."

"The world wouldn't let that happen."

"You're right," Shehan said, a knowing look in his eyes. "They'd kill us all first."

"It must be a lie," I insisted. The idea had horrified me last night, and I didn't like it any better now, but I would've done anything to stop the virus reaching my dad in Canada. "But the theory about the aliens carrying ADS could be right." The raindrops were falling more quickly. A quick succession of them pelted my cheek and neck.

"It's too big a coincidence," Shehan agreed. "But what do we do now?" We stood outside in the rain talking it over and decided to tell Ciara the news and let her make up her mind whether Adam should know. Then the three of us would have to work out whether it was safe to stay where we were.

When we got back to the house, Ciara and Adam were still asleep. Adam woke up first. He was hungry and feeling better, but we only gave him one slice of bread, to be on the safe side. He didn't waste any time in asking about the body, and I lied and told him that it was gone. "The men must've come back for whatever it was," Shehan added, the two of us acting perplexed.

As soon as Ciara came downstairs I took her aside and confessed everything we knew. Her face went almost as ashy as the alien's had been. "You did the right thing in not telling Adam," she told me. "We have to keep him away from the radio so he won't hear anything about it."

"But one of us needs to listen," I said. I volunteered to be the one to listen for updates while Shehan and Ciara kept Adam distracted by making him help gather containers from the front room and kitchen and leave them out in the yard to catch rainwater.

Uneasy as the disembodied voices and the creepy things they had to say about the infected made me, listening to the radio also made me feel like I was actually doing something. Knowledge is power, Mr. Nishiada used to say.

At first I couldn't find anyone offering solid information, but at nine o'clock RTE began broadcasting and issued a boil water advisory, fearing imminent failure at water treatment facilities. I would've sworn the girl reading the news wasn't any older than eighteen. These days young people were the only ones still in their right minds. The girl warned people to steer clear of groups of the infected because ADS sufferers were more dangerous in great numbers. She said the danger was worse in the Dublin area because the 3Arena medical base had been breached. With their limited resources, RTE couldn't confirm the breach, but members of the public had told them that most of the patients had run off on foot after overpowering military personnel at the site.

There couldn't be much military might left, and not many medical people either, and I wondered if the breach at the 3 Arena base would be followed by one at the RDS.

As soon as the RTE news was finished I started moving the dial around. That's when I heard it — a trio of teenagers who said they'd found a dead alien body in Malahide.

"It'd floated into the marina and was bobbing in the water by a boat," one of the boys declared. "I know people won't want to believe us, but if you've seen one of them too you'll know what we're saying is the truth. It was long and gray, not small like some of the aliens you see in films. This thing had a massive head and eyes and a face that looked more like an animal's."

A girl interrupted him to say, "We've heard some other people on the radio talk about the aliens too. We've never seen a live one, but we've heard they move dead fast and don't make contact with humans. So far no one really knows why they're here — and if they brought the virus with them or not — but if you're listening to this, don't take any chances with the live ones. Keep your distance. We don't know what they're capable of."

Had the thing been stalking us before it died? I shut the radio off and went to tell Shehan and Ciara what I'd heard.

The two of them plus Adam were in the kitchen, huddled over a Risk board. At the sight of me, Ciara said, "Adam, why don't you go take a shower?"

For once he didn't argue with her. Ten seconds after Adam had left the room Ciara swallowed hard, her fingernails scraping at the streaky remains of her nail polish. "Don't worry," I assured her. "There was nothing really awful about the aliens."

Or anything good either. I began summing up the RTE report, Ciara wincing at the news about the medical base. As I repeated the story about the dead alien in Malahide she asked, "What can they want? Why are they here?"

I didn't know the answer to that any more than she did. "If it was an invasion, they wouldn't be hiding the way they are," I replied slowly. *Unless they were waiting for something.* Reinforcements, maybe. Those last two thoughts I kept to myself. Why scare anyone with more crazy theories?

With Adam safely in the shower, the three of us voted against relocating until we knew more. We should've been taking advantage of the light by gathering supplies from neighbor's houses, but we were too freaked out to leave the house. If there weren't ADS-infected lurking, ready to pounce, it was something worse.

I wrote down what had happened so far today, my breath quickening when I had to describe the thing across the street. Only when Adam and Ripley started getting restless indoors and Adam pointed out the break in the rain did I get my nerve up enough to risk going into the backyard. Adam had a pretty good arm, and we took turns tossing the ball to each other and then Ripley.

"I'm glad you're feeling better," I told him, my ears extra alert for any strange noises on the wind. "I guess we overdid it with the food last night." What if the *thing* had friends? What if they were angry with us for disturbing its body? And what about the men we'd seen last night? Or the woman we'd left at the bottom of my grandparents' stairs?

"The french fries were okay," Adam said. "But everything else tasted so dodgy that I can't believe I'm the only one who was sick."

"Come on, it wasn't that bad." I hurled the ball past Ripley, who took off after it like she was aiming to win a race against a thoroughbred.

"It was so," he insisted.

"You must be one of those picky eater kids, huh?" I didn't say it quite like Ciara would've, but I guess I was starting to understand why she got so aggravated with him.

Ripley plopped the ball down at my feet. Adam bounded over to the ball and threw it in the direction of the back fence, his face stubborn. "Not that much."

"So, a little," I teased. "Anyway, it's not like we have much fresh food left. Just what your parents had in their cooler."

"That's okay by me." A fleeting grin skated across Adam's face. "Why are you friends with Ciara anyway? You seem okay."

I tilted my head. "She's okay too. She took care of you last night, didn't she?" I knew she had, I was just trying to prove my point.

"Only because there was no one else." Adam glanced down at the mucky ball Ripley had delivered to him. "We have different mothers, you know."

"I know. But regular siblings fight too. That's how they are." From what I'd seen of my friends and their siblings, that was pretty true.

"You don't have any, how would you know?" Adam said accusingly.

There he went being annoying again, and I shrugged and motioned for him to throw me the ball. We tossed it back and forth in silence until the clouds started spitting rain. For once I was happy about the weather; it meant I could go back inside where it was safer.

But when I got there — half-expecting to stumble on Ciara and Shehan with their arms around each other — I found Shehan in the front room alone, labeling boxes and containers and jotting down a master list of everything we owned. "I'm going to head next door with Ripley and see if they have anything we can use," he announced.

The house on the left was one whose door had been left wide open, and that made me uneasy. *Anything* could've gotten inside. Ripley would sniff out any threats and warn him, but I knew how quickly things could go wrong. "You're not going anywhere alone," I said. "We already talked about that."

"I wouldn't be alone," Shehan pointed out. "I'd be with Ripley. More of those things could show up anytime. Or those guys from last night. There might be something next door that could help us."

"I get it." Weapons. Staying in Shehan's house or yard wouldn't necessarily stop anything bad from happening to us. We needed to prepare. "But you know how this works — safety in numbers. We should all go this time."

"You win." Doubt skimmed across Shehan's face. "I guess it can't hurt to have more of us to carry whatever supplies we can find."

Or for him not to have to take risks alone. I wanted to make him promise me he'd stop thinking it was up to him to protect the rest of us and to point out that he needed protecting too. But the feeling behind the words felt too heavy; I couldn't trust the syllables to come out right.

"I'll get Ciara and Adam," I volunteered. Rushing through the house, I ran into Ciara in the hall, her lips curled in frustration. "What is it?"

"Just Adam being Adam." She bit her tongue. "Never mind, you look like you're in a hurry. Did something happen?"

I explained about the plan to drop in next door.

"Good idea." She screwed up her eyes, her cheeks flaring. "I'll go tell Adam."

I joined Shehan in the front room again, the two of us pacing in front of our heap of supplies, restless to get the trip over with. Then a noise from upstairs interrupted our silence — the sound of Ciara and Adam arguing at the top of their lungs. "Déjà vu," I said dryly. "Do you and Sara fight like that?"

A smile pulled at Shehan's cheeks. "Sometimes, yeah. More when I was younger and acting the maggot."

"Acting the maggot," I repeated, grinning back. "Some of the stuff you Irish people say kills me."

Shehan's eyes filled with familiar mischief. "*You Aaaye-rish people kill me*," he echoed, flattening his voice out so it approximated a male version of mine. Right away I missed the lilt of his accent. "You're such a Yank."

It wasn't the first time I'd heard him say that. Years ago I'd been sure to correct him, stressing that I was Canadian, not American. But now I knew he was just kidding around.

It felt as if we could stand there teasing each other all day, if only Ciara and Adam weren't making so much noise. One — or maybe both — of them was stomping around like a T. Rex. It wouldn't have surprised me if bits of the ceiling had started falling in on Shehan and me.

"Adam says he won't come along," Ciara cried, barreling into the front room with us. "I swear I could wring his neck."

"I guess you should just stay here with him, then," I told her. Shehan nodded next to me.

"Leave me alone, Ciara!" Adam hollered from upstairs where he must have been listening. "I don't want you here. Ripley can stay with me."

"*Right*," Ciara said sarcastically, but only loud enough for Shehan and me to hear. "Why would Ripley want to do that?" Ciara's voice returned to ordinary volume. "Look, you two take Ripley. If there's anyone next door you need to worry about, she'll sniff them out."

Minutes later Shehan, Ripley, and I crept into the house next door like robbers, which I guess we sort of were. Ciara was watching from the open front door of Shehan's house. Ripley remained calm and quiet as Shehan and I hovered inside the entranceway. I stepped outside for a second, waving at Ciara to let her know we were safe. She nodded gratefully and waved back.

Ignoring how wrong it felt to be in someone else's house, I ducked inside again and wandered through the hall. The living room was pretty old-fashioned with dark wood cabinets and side tables and pieces of furniture sort of like ones I'd heard decorators on TV describe as "Empire."

Someone had left a blue plaid blanket on the couch, but other than that, the place looked tidy. In the corner of the room a grandfather clock was ticking away, marking each second as it passed. The noise drew my eyes to the clock and then a nearby birdcage. At first I thought it was empty, but no, a pair of gorgeous blue and green lovebirds lined the bottom of the cage.

"They must've died from dehydration," Shehan noted from behind me, crossing over to the cage.

I felt myself frown. "I guess we should've come over sooner." We continued prowling the deserted house, opening drawers and tugging items off shelves. "Who lived here?" I asked.

"Mr. and Mrs. O'Halloran. Your grandparents knew them too. They've been here since before my family moved in." Shehan turned to look at the birdcage again. "Ciara would know them as well. At least enough to say hello."

The O'Hallorans had a bunch of photo albums, and I made the mistake of opening one. My gaze jumped to a faded old snapshot of a pretty woman in her thirties, sun shining in her eyes as she sat outside on a lawn chair with a pouting baby on her lap. Did that baby have ADS now too, or had the person it had grown into moved across the ocean somewhere safe?

I slammed the album shut and announced that I was moving into the kitchen. Not only did it have fewer reminders of the people who had lived here, but it had more things we needed. Except for a decent-looking head of cauliflower, I didn't trust the food left in the fridge, but there were so many cans of soup on the kitchen shelves that I had to wonder if the O'Hallorans ever ate much else. I ended up with sixteen soup cans, a bunch of cans of veggies, two cans of meatballs in gravy, a can of beef and ale stew dumplings, and a weird-looking can of hot dogs in brine. I even scooped up the really boring stuff like stock cubes, gravy in a can, tea bags, and blackcurrant jam.

Shehan found two more flashlights and extra batteries, matches, and candles, and I hauled a "sun oven" out from a storage cupboard under the stairs. "It looks like they never even opened it," I said excitedly. "But according to the packaging you don't need any electricity to cook with it. You leave the oven outside with the food inside it, and the sun does the cooking on its own."

We gobbled down a bunch of the O'Hallorans' custard cream cookies in celebration. Even Ripley got two.

Neither of us wanted to go into the bedrooms (potentially too creepy), but we headed up to the main bathroom together and sorted through the O'Hallorans' medicine cabinet. There was something Shehan thought was a prescription-strength painkiller as well as chewable pills for diarrhea. "With the kinds of stuff we'll be eating, we might need them," I said, sliding the medication into one of the cloth bags I'd grabbed from the storage cupboard.

Shehan tossed some multivitamins into the bag, and we were wrapping up our search when a door slammed. Footsteps thumped rapidly up the stairs towards us. I jumped, picturing the woman from my grandparents' attic. My scalp was still tender where she'd grabbed my hair.

My eyes zipped to the open bathroom door, fear chugging through my veins. From here we could only make out the top of the staircase. So far the view was clear, but the noise was closing in fast.

Suddenly Ciara materialized in front of us, taking the last few steps of the staircase two at a time. "You two have to —" She froze mid-sentence as she read our expressions. Her jaw and cheeks rearranged themselves into a guilty smile. "Sorry! Didn't mean to scare you. I just didn't want you to miss it."

"Miss what?" Shehan asked, his voice cracking.

Ciara squeezed into the bathroom with us. She pointed out the window that overlooked the O'Hallorans' back-yard. A medium-sized rustic garden shed framed by two tall trees sat at the far end of the yard. Dread leapt into my throat as I registered movement outside. *Not again.* I wasn't ready to deal with another extraterrestrial threat.

Luckily, there wasn't one. Instead, a silvery-black monkey with Mohawk hair perched in one of the high branches of the tree on the left. I laughed fast and sharp, the relief pinching at my sides. "That's wild." *Literally.*

Ciara laughed along with me, partially losing her breath. "It's, like, a whole tribe of them or something."

I'd spotted the solo one first, but sure enough, four other monkeys were reclining on the lawn. One had a baby nestled against her, its casual but alert eyes staring across the yard. Another monkey was lying spread out on the grass — the picture of relaxation — while the fourth monkey picked through the hair on the prone monkey's arm, grooming him or her, I guessed. The whole thing was such a bizarrely magical sight that the three of us paused and watched in silence for a minute.

Of all the weird things I'd seen in the past few days, this was the best — a real-life nature show happening practically in our own backyard. "Isn't it unbelievable?" I whispered, although I doubted the monkeys could hear us indoors and must have been used to human noises anyway.

Shehan nodded slowly, like he didn't have any other words to describe it.

"They're macaques," Ciara said as we stood close together ogling the silver-black Mohawk monkeys. "I don't know what kind, but I remember them from the last time I was at the zoo. The tour guide said they're hunted for meat and that people eat them for Christmas in some places."

"Will I go out and grab one, then?" Shehan smiled, cocking his head at the window. "We can try it in the sun oven."

Ciara smirked. "I'd love to see you try."

"Me too," I chimed. "I bet they'd tear you to pieces. Either that or make you their human slave — force you to do all their grooming and food gathering."

"I reckon you're right," Shehan agreed, still grinning. "Lots of hairstyling and trips to Tesco's." Our eyes caught on each other's, sort of like when you trip over your own feet, and I felt my face begin to heat up.

I pointed my gaze through the glass again. It was amazing the protective vibe the mother monkey cast around the baby. Almost like a human mom.

"I better get back," Ciara said, regret curdling in her throat. "I ran Ripley next door to play guard dog for Adam before coming up." Ciara had probably only been gone for less than three minutes, and I couldn't blame her for being reluctant to leave our view of the macaques.

"Did you show Adam the monkeys?" I asked.

She nodded quickly. "I thought it might make him change his mind and want to come over. But he's still sulking — sulking and watching them from our bedroom window at the same time. He pointed out they have lions, tigers, a snow leopard, and a crocodile at the zoo too. He said they were the only things that would attack us, probably."

I erupted into a laugh, although that wasn't really funny either. All we had to worry about was the electricity being down, blackout flu sufferers raging in mobs, alien creatures, and a few wild animals from the Dublin Zoo. Wow, we almost had it easy.

Ciara shuffled down the steps, Shehan and I following close behind. After she'd gone we wandered back into the kitchen, giving every nook and cranny a second look in case we'd missed something important — a handgun or pepper spray canister. On impulse I picked up the phone, checking for a dial tone.

I should've known better. Shehan slipped into the kitchen and saw my expression as I replaced the receiver. "I just thought I'd try," I said slowly.

Next to me, Shehan was quiet. His stare, as I hung up the phone, was so sympathetic that it made me feel weaker.

"It might still come back," he told me. "We should keep trying and trying."

I massaged my temples and squeezed my eyes shut to stop the tears before they started. When I opened them again, Shehan was still staring, his fingers brushing against my hand. "We'll be all right," he said. "We have enough supplies to keep us going for a long time. And we don't have any reason to think those *things* would try to hurt us."

Calling them *things* instead of *aliens* didn't make them any less scary.

"I know." I frowned at him, pretending to be braver than I was. "You don't always have to act like such a guy, you know. You've lost as much as I have. You can fall apart every once in a while."

Shehan raised his eyebrows, weariness clouding his hazel eyes. "You never do. And anyway, what good would that do?"

None, I guess.

"It's not a competition," he added. "We don't have to out-tough each other, do we?" Close as he already was, he stepped nearer to me, one of his hands sliding over the back of my head, tracing the natural curl of my hair down my back.

I melted in a way that pushed me closer to breaking, but closer to something I wanted too. "What're you doing?" I asked, my voice as warm as the rest of me.

"Sorry." He snatched his hand back. "It's just hard to see you sad and keep my distance."

I nodded slightly, as though that explained nearly everything. "But Ciara … if she came back in she might get the wrong idea."

"Ciara?" Shehan tilted his head like he'd heard me wrong. "What does she have to do with anything?"

"You and her." I was irritated with him for making me

spell it out. "You know ..."

"I don't know." Shehan jammed his hands into his pockets. When he stared at me with those infinite amber eyes, they made me feel like something extra. Still Naomi at the core, but better, more. "Ciara and I are just friends. Why should she care what you and I do?"

"But ..." My head was still swirling with sadness and disappointment. I couldn't put my thoughts together. "I saw you together in your front room."

A look of recognition slunk across Shehan's face.

"And I'm not going to do this to her," I continued. No matter how much I liked Shehan, it wasn't right. "Neither should you."

"I'm not doing anything to her. I told you, Ciara and I are friends. That's all." I watched Shehan exhale. "What you saw was just us making up. After you walked off she was still ready to claw my eyes out at first — more angry with me than she'd been with Adam. But we patched it up because you were right, we shouldn't be arguing. There's no sense fighting about little things when the world's gone mad around us." Shehan chewed his lower lip, the two of us still only about a foot and a half apart. "I don't like Ciara like that. I like *you*. Before any of this happened, but more now." He looked down at the telephone, almost shy. "I shouldn't be saying this, with everything going on. I almost came out with it after you were attacked by the sick woman in your gran's house. Watching her come after you like that was horrible."

Shehan stopped dead, his eyes trapping mine. Then his lips parted slowly again, as though it took some effort to do it. "I don't want anything to happen to you."

"I don't want anything to happen to you either." The admission felt like hot sauce on my tongue. Somehow, now that Shehan had come out and said he and Ciara weren't together, I wasn't really surprised. It was like a part of me had known the truth all along. "I'm glad you told me. I'm just ..." Relieved. Jumpy. Pining for my parents, one of them thousands of miles away and the other possibly within walking distance but just as unreachable. Every hour felt like a new challenge.

"Yeah, I know." Shehan took a step back, giving me space.

On impulse I jumped forward to close the gap, wrapping my arms around him. This time he hugged me back — firmly, but gently at the same time — and although the timing was wrong, a sliver of happiness squeezed sideways into my heart. It wasn't like any hug I'd ever had before. It felt like California sunshine.

"We should probably start taking stuff back to my house," Shehan said when we pulled away from each other. "But ..." He tilted towards me, his lips grazing mine. I barely had time to feel the kiss. I'd never had anyone's lips on mine before, and I wished I could've had that first kiss at my birthday barbecue instead, someplace quiet after Shehan had given me the card in the purple envelope. I would've been able to concentrate on the moment more. It would've just been a happy thing without being all mixed up with sad and scary ones.

But this was better than it not happening at all. I threaded my fingers through Shehan's and pulled him towards the front door with me, the two of us gathering our new supplies together before rushing back to where we'd left Ciara and Adam.

FOURTEEN

WE TOOK EVERYTHING we needed in two trips, adding it to our stash in Shehan's front room. Ciara and Ripley were waiting for us there, but Adam still wouldn't come down when we all shouted for him. "He's still holed up in the bedroom," Ciara explained. "Probably still ogling the monkeys." While Shehan continued with his inventory list, Ciara and I invented a supermarket-type system, sorting the shelf-stable food into seven categories.

My eyes kept snagging on Shehan across the room, the memory of what had happened between us in the O'Hallorans' kitchen making my stomach flutter. If Ciara sensed what was happening between Shehan and me, I couldn't tell. With all of us living together, I didn't want to make things awkward for anyone, but keeping it a secret wasn't right either.

We were getting near the end of the job — and I still hadn't worked out what to say — when Ciara started sniffling, and then sneezing. "I'm allergic to dust," she sputtered, covering her nose with both hands. "Some of the cans and packages aren't the newest." There were plenty of tissues and toilet paper in the front room with us, but we were rationing supplies, and Ciara didn't want to open a new package until we had to. She chased one of her allergy pills from the medicine box down with a gulp of rainwater we'd gathered from the backyard and went upstairs to grab tissues from the bathroom.

Alone again, Shehan reached for my hand, squeezing it as he asked, "Are you okay?"

He must have been referring to my moment with the phone, and I gripped his hand back. "I'm trying not to think too much."

"Me too," he admitted. "I wish my mind had an off switch. Want to head outside for a bit? Distract ourselves?" In the distance we could hear Ciara still blowing her nose.

We hurried into the yard together. Shehan checked for the macaques by hauling himself on top of the fence and scouring the yards in either direction. "It looks like they've moved on," he announced.

Too bad. I liked the idea of having monkey neighbors much better than ADS-stricken or alien ones. To entertain ourselves, Shehan and I moved the water containers out of our way and kicked a soccer ball around like we used to. Even as I struggled to keep up with him, my energy level surged. Sometimes it only takes one good thing to change your mood. Seeing the monkeys earlier had reminded me that even here and now, our lives could be about more than being scared.

It was a long while until either of us wanted to take a break, and when we finally did Shehan said, "When things calm down I'll take you to the club and we can play snooker."

I noticed that he'd said *when* instead of *if*, and I resolved to say it like that from now on — act like I one hundred percent believed this would be over any day now. "When things calm down I want homemade mushroom manicotti and garlic bread," I told him, licking my lips at the thought. "I'll get my dad to bake us some. He makes amazing pasta, but his manicotti is the best. So cheesy delicious."

My mind dashed off a quick mental list:

FAVORITE FOODS
- Nanaimo-bar pie — my brain gets a little sugar high jolt just thinking about it
- Sweet potato fries
- Vegetable paella — which I know is not the way some people like it but I don't like most fish but I still love paella
- Manicotti — especially the way my dad makes it (what he calls his secret recipe)
- Strawberries
- Bananas
- Ham & cheese quesadillas
- Zucchini and rice pancakes — so crispy and amazing
- Broccoli — even plain

"That sounds brilliant." Shehan's hazel eyes gleamed. "And will he mind, do you think? About us, I mean."

I didn't have a chance to answer — the sky ripped open with such force that you'd think someone had slashed at the clouds with a razor blade. Rain whipped down, sending Shehan and I scurrying for the door. Before we could reach it, a cold-blooded shriek tore after us, shattering the air. We cowered in unison, the two of us turning in the direction of the noise. There was nothing to see; the fence blocked our view. Shehan came to his senses first. He pulled me inside, my hair drenched and our faces pinched with fear.

"Upstairs!" I shouted. We raced up the steps and into Shehan's bedroom. He pulled the curtain back, revealing a view of the parkland beyond the fence. The storm clouds overhead had turned the landscape dark and wet. About fifty feet away, three men surrounded a towering figure in clinging black. Its head was as enormous as its limbs were long. I already knew what the thing looked like underneath its protective second skin, that it was no man or woman. The thing wasn't gliding like the one had the first time I'd spotted one. Its movements were slow and labored, as though it were wounded. The men closed in, roaring like animals and raising their fists.

The alien's mechanical squeal curled my toes. The sound could've been fear, or it could've been anger; my ears couldn't tell the difference. The thing's back was to us, and the men's fists rammed into its body, the squeal intensifying. One of the men appeared to levitate in front of the alien, the man's feet kicking frenziedly at nothing. Then the man began to shake, like a puppet on a string — faster and faster, until he collapsed motionless on the grass. A second man was still pummeling the alien. The third man turned and ran, his scream mixing with the alien's squeal.

Inside Shehan's room, a hand gripped my shoulder. "What's going on?" Ciara cried from behind me.

In the seconds that I turned to look at her, I missed the end of the altercation down below. When I swung back to the window, two men instead of one lay crumpled on the ground. The third was hurrying away, not looking back, and the alien had vanished.

I numbly explained what we'd seen, Ciara staring out the window, speechless.

"Are they ... are they dead?" she said finally.

"We don't know," Shehan replied.

But they still weren't moving. Meanwhile, the three of us fell into a sort of shock. Our situation had worsened again. Now we knew that we had every reason to be afraid of the aliens, that they could easily match and outdo human violence. "Where's Adam?" I mumbled. He and Ripley should've been standing here with us — how could they not have heard the commotion outside?

"Still in the bedroom, I guess." Ciara's eyes popped. "I've been giving him space. I fell asleep on the couch for a bit. I was tired from being up with him last night." She backed swiftly out of the room, Shehan and I following her. "I haven't seen him since I told him about the monkeys."

Ciara's face scrunched up as she bellowed her brother's name, then Ripley's. The three of us kept moving, first into the master bedroom, then Sara's, Mr. Ranaweera's office, and the bathroom. Ripley was good about coming when she was called, and the fact that she hadn't already appeared made us move more quickly, dashing downstairs where we each bound into a different room to search for her and Adam.

We met in the ground floor hallway seconds later, out of luck. "Maybe he went next door after all," I said.

"Or back to our house!" Ciara exclaimed, whirling towards the front door.

"Wait!" I yelled after her. "We should stick together. We don't know what happened to him."

"You think he was taken?" Ciara's voice was hoarse. A loose lock of her hair dipped into one of her eyes. "You think one of those things got him when I was over at the O'Hallorans'?"

Shehan forced his wet hair back with his fingers. "Probably not — you were only gone a couple of minutes, and Ripley would've put up a fight. But it's more dangerous to split up."

Together the three of us sprinted to the O'Hallorans' house and then Ciara's, looking over our shoulders and listening for the sound of aliens. There was no trace of Adam or Ripley in either place, and although Adam wasn't my brother — half or otherwise — I was more frightened than I'd been since the moment Mom had run off. Adam could've been anywhere by now. Shehan and I had been in the backyard for at least an hour.

We didn't have the luxury of worrying about being spotted by aliens or sick people lurking — we tore up and down the street, calling for Adam and Ripley so loudly that my voice was in shreds and my clothes plastered to my body from the pelting rain. "This is my fault," Ciara choked out, fighting a sob. "He ran away. Now he's out there with those things and thousands of sick people. I should never have gone next door."

"It's not your fault," I countered. "He could have run off anyway. Anytime we weren't within a few feet of him."

"He was doing my head in." Ciara's hands rushed to her face. "I should've checked on him again after I came back, but I was glad for some time on my own. He thinks I hate him. He said so."

There was no time for blame. "Where would he go?" I asked, oxygen swept from my lungs. "*Think.*" No matter what, we had to find Adam. I'd told Shehan I didn't want anything to happen to him, but I couldn't stand the thought of losing Ciara or Adam either. The four of us were all each other had. We'd become almost like family. Being with the three of them had gotten me through this up till now.

"I don't know," Ciara croaked. Our faces were so wet that her tears disappeared into the rain. You wouldn't have been able to tell she'd been crying except that her eyes were lined with pink. "His mom's house in Sutton, maybe."

"Sutton?" Shehan repeated. "It'd take at least four hours to walk to Sutton from here." For my benefit he explained, "It's on the Northside. At the coast, near Howth."

"He could've taken his bike," Ciara said. "My dad brought it over here from his mom's house so he could use it this summer." We hurried back to the Kavanaghs' place, where Ciara headed directly for the backyard shed. "It's gone! That's it — he must be cycling home."

"We'll take the car and go after him," I said urgently. "C'mon."

Seconds later we were squeezing into Mr. Ranaweera's

sedan, Shehan in the driver's seat on the right and Ciara next to him. I leaned forward, against her seat, and we sped out of the driveway and into the road. Shehan was years too young for a driver's license, but he must've driven before because the car didn't lurch or anything. As we turned onto Birchwood Street, the emptiness of the suburban-looking environment was broken by the sight of a man in a torn navy windbreaker sitting on the sidewalk, holding an open umbrella over his head. With his face obscured by his hood I couldn't be sure, but my guess was that it was the same man I'd run into when my mom had fled.

"Stop the car!" I cried, pointing. "Maybe he's seen something."

Shehan hit the brakes. "You know he probably has blackout flu. He could be dangerous, and he probably won't be able to tell us anything."

"That depends on how long sick people can remember for. It's worth a try." I pushed the car door open, Shehan and Ciara scrambling outside after me.

As I neared the man, I noticed a cup of tea between his legs. It was steaming, still warm. Did people with ADS remember how to brew themselves cups of tea? From what I'd seen and heard, it seemed unlikely. The urge to eat wouldn't disappear, but any idea about how to use small appliances would've been blacked out.

"Hello," I called to the man, trying to sound as cheerful and unthreatening as possible; I didn't want to get attacked again.

As he stared up at me I got a good look at his wispy

beard and bald head. It was the same man who'd taunted me the night the soldiers had taken my mom away. He had a devilish look in his eyes, as though it was a point of pride for him to irritate everyone he spoke to. The man clearly wasn't one of the bad. To me he didn't seem blank or blissed, either. He defied categorization. It gave me a weird kind of hope to know maybe my mom hadn't been going *bad* when she ran off. Even turning out like this man would be better than that.

"We lost a little boy about nine years old," I said, knowing that the man wouldn't remember me. "He was on a bike and had a big dog with him. Have you seen anyone like that?"

"He was wearing a Spider-Man hoodie," Ciara said, the three of us standing in a tight knot in front of the man as continuous lashings of rainwater chilled our skin.

"Spider-what?" the man asked, raising his tea to his lips.

"He doesn't know anything," Shehan said impatiently. "Let's go."

"*You* don't know anything," the man retorted. "You're a fidget gobby thing if I ever saw one." He snorted and swallowed a big gulp of tea.

"I know it's not their fault they're sick, but all these people infected with blackout flu are wrecking my head," Shehan said, staring off down the street like we were wasting our time.

"So, you haven't seen him?" I asked, not giving up yet.

"I did see him." The man fondled his beard. "With his furry thing and wheels, he was, whispering down the road."

"He doesn't make a lot of sense," a nearby male voice declared. "But he does know some things, sometimes." My gaze jerked instantly to the source of the words. A young man, around twenty years old, was standing in the open doorway of the house next door, eyeing us cautiously.

"We're looking for a nine-year-old boy on a bike," Shehan said. "He went missing up to an hour ago."

"I have not seen a boy," the man replied. His English was good, but I heard an accent — Japanese, probably, since that's how he looked. "We found a young girl when we walked along the street around the corner yesterday. Much younger than the boy you're looking for."

"Which street?" I asked. Was this one of the men I'd spotted last night?

"Just there — Sykes Close." He motioned to my gran and granddad's street as a South Asian guy, roughly the same age, joined him in the doorway. A little blond girl in a denim jumpsuit clung to the neck of the second man, one of her thumbs in her mouth. "We were out looking for a friend who is sick with the thing they call blackout flu. We never found him, but this little girl ran out into the road when she heard us. She'd been abandoned for days, it seems, and was living by her wits in the house alone."

The little girl must've lived at the far end of Sykes Close. We'd never heard a peep from her, and since we'd been keeping a fairly low profile, I guess she'd never heard or seen us either.

"That's the same street we live on," I told them. If we couldn't trust two guys who would take in a toddler and treat her like their own daughter, we couldn't trust anyone. "We heard you out there, but things have been so dangerous — we didn't know whether you were safe to talk to. Did you see the thing down beside the bush?" They must've. That must've been part of what all their shouting was about.

"The alien," the man holding the girl replied, frowning deeply. "We saw it. It was barely breathing. They say there are more of them, but I didn't believe any of it until I saw for myself. They say they brought the blackout flu with them."

"We've heard that too," Shehan said. "And we know for a fact there are more of them." We exchanged names with the men — who were Daniel and Anish — and Shehan quickly explained what we'd seen beyond his yard.

"We heard the noise," Anish said, frowning. "We didn't know that's what it was. From what you say, maybe it's not safe here. But then, where is?" Anish told us he and Daniel had come to Ireland for summer English classes and had been feeding the bearded man each day but hadn't been able to convince him to take shelter indoors. "He seems harmless," Anish added. "Not like some of the others."

I wish I'd opened the door when I'd heard Daniel and Anish in the street the night before. It helped to know there were people like them still out here, but we didn't have time to stay and talk. With every second Adam could be farther away.

We said goodbye to Daniel and Anish, gave them Shehan's address, and told them we hoped to meet up with them again very soon. "You just keep carting the way you were," the bearded ADS-infected man shouted after us as we walked to the car. "That's the direction your spider friend went off in."

The entire encounter hadn't taken more than five minutes, but Shehan sped down Birchwood Street to make up for it. We shot onto Haverhill Road, my heart in my mouth as I took in the scene. A single burnt-out double-decker bus with two flat tires squatted forlornly by the curb. There had been four buses the last time I'd been here. Was this one of them? Abandoned cars peppered the road, some of them fatally singed too and others simply abandoned. The Spar and every other shop front we could see had been broken into and emptied out. Jagged glass glazed the street along with scattered garbage, rotting food, and lumps of wet fabric that someone had probably worn once upon a time. A pack of six or seven dogs of various breeds and sizes roamed the deserted street, restless and dazed. They weren't used to having to take care of themselves; I knew what that felt like.

Shehan slowed to a crawl so he could maneuver around the cars. The area looked like a war zone. Everything was muddy, broken, or decomposing. My eyes temporarily forgot to scan for Adam; they were in shock like the rest of me. It hadn't looked this desolate out on the main road when I'd followed Mom here days ago. Either the aliens or the ADS-infected had destroyed it.

"Look!" Ciara screamed. "Adam's hoodie."

We'd hardly been moving in the first place, so Shehan barely had to tap the brakes. About thirty feet to our right, in front of a scorched mailbox, a pot-bellied middle-aged

man in a T-shirt streaked with purple goo was tossing a
boy into the pavement, face first. We didn't need to see the
boy's face to know it was Adam — the Spider-Man figure
on the back of his red hoodie told us that — and the three
of us leapt out of the car and ran towards him. Shehan
charged into the pot-bellied man with maximum force,
easily toppling him to the ground. Ciara and I were just
seconds behind, but by the time the guy in the Spider-Man
hoodie rolled over each of us had already realized it wasn't
Adam. It wasn't even a child, just a very small man —
short, with an extremely lean build and grizzly moustache.

"Where'd you get this?" Ciara shouted, bending over
him and pointing at a hoodie sleeve. "Did you see the
little boy who was wearing it? Where'd he go?"

The man wearing Adam's hoodie — or one just like
it — stared blandly at Ciara. Then he bounded to his feet
and ran off up the road, the pack of dogs careening excitedly after him. Shehan stood too, the pot-bellied man he'd
tackled glaring at him as though he'd like to return the
favor. "You knocked me over," the man said accusingly.
"What are you doing here, anyway? Who are you?"

"Who are *you*?" I asked, lobbing the question back at him.

The man switched his attention to me. "Don't speak to
me that way, girly. I could break you in two."

"We're just looking for my brother," Ciara cut in,
standing close to me. "We're really sorry. We thought that
was him you were beating up."

"I wasn't beating up anyone. What're you on about?"
The man grew more wild-eyed with every word. "Who are
you? Who sent you here?"

"No one." I took a long step back as the man rose, Ciara in lockstep with me and Shehan clambering to my side. "We're just *kids*. We're looking for her brother."

"Kids? You're too old to be kids." The man stretched out his finger and poked at my shoulder as if testing my claim.

"Don't touch her," Shehan warned.

"And don't you threaten me, boyo. I'll touch who I want, whenever I want." The man's face reddened as he craned his neck forward. "Who did you say you were, anyway? How do you know each other?"

"We're friends," I replied staunchly. "We've known each other for years."

"For years," he repeated, sneering. "Well, isn't that a fine thing. And me here on my own not remembering a soul. What makes the three of you so special that you can remember things?"

"*Get in the car,*" Shehan said to Ciara and me, his tone calm but his face taut. "We need to get out of here."

We turned at the same moment, and I was ready to sprint for the car — we were all pretty fast, we should've been able to outrun the man no problem — only I couldn't move because his beefy hands had clamped down on my shoulders.

Shehan whirled to face him, drew his fist back, and sent it shooting into the man's nose. I heard the crunch of it breaking and felt the man's hands leave me. Ciara was steps ahead, already partway to the car, and I was about to hurtle forward when the man punched Shehan square in the stomach. Shehan fell backwards into the street, dropping like a bowling pin. My head flinched as his struck the pavement.

I'd been in fights before, but not for a couple of years and only with boys my age; I knew I was no match for the rabid, red-faced man kicking at Shehan on the ground, but I didn't have a choice. Twisting around, I angled to kick the man in the nuts as he continued to drive his foot into Shehan's side.

It was what my dad had always told me to do if a guy tried to grab me, go for the nuts or Adam's apple, which-ever was in easier reach. I'd been so stunned by the woman in my grandparents' attic that I'd forgotten the advice. This time I remembered, and I hurled my right foot into the vulnerable spot between the man's legs, throwing all my weight, all my energy, and all my anger into the motion.

The man's shoulders and chest caved in to the pain, sagging inward as he bent at the waist, groaning. His posture reminded me of a roly-poly bug when they tucked into a ball to protect themselves, only the red-faced man was still standing. Ciara, who had run back towards us, took care of that. She shoved the man hard from behind, sending him plummeting down next to Shehan.

I hurried to Shehan's side to help him up, Ciara stum-bling over to his other side. Shehan winced as we got him on his feet, clearly in pain. He couldn't run. We had to walk him gingerly, but swiftly, to the car. I turned back to glance at our attacker. He'd rolled onto his side and was lifting his head off the ground to watch us go. Another minute and he'd probably be ready to stand.

We were almost at the car now anyway. We'd make it.

Only the car wasn't empty like it should've been. While we'd been fighting off the roly-poly man, three women in their thirties had climbed inside. One in the front seat and two in the back. If they were bad like the man, we were in trouble.

I swung the front door open and shouted, "Get out of our car! It doesn't belong to you."

Ciara opened the back door, leaving Shehan leaning against the hood of the car. "Out!" she repeated, staring harshly at the women in the back seat. "We need to go."

The women may as well have been crash test dummies. They stared hazily back at us, none of them making a move to leave the car. At least they weren't bad, just blank. But the roly-poly man wouldn't stay down forever, and as I was turning to look at him again, a voice rang out from somewhere above us: "*Run!*"

FIFTEEN

THE WHITE-HAIRED MAN leaned out a second-storey window, over the remnants of a hairdresser's shop, screaming feverishly down at us. My eyes singled him out in a flash. He looked terrified. "There's a horde coming!" he bellowed. "They're just round the bend in the road. You don't want to be standing there when they arrive."

A horde like we'd heard about on the radio. Much more dangerous in great numbers, they'd said. I'd already seen enough danger — I didn't want first-hand proof of how bad they could be — and I poked my head into the car again and screeched at the women.

Desperate, Ciara grabbed the arm of the woman closest to her and tried to wrench her into the street. The woman was as strong as an ox. She gritted her teeth and pulled back in the opposite direction, propelling Ciara farther into the car.

"There's no time for that!" the man hollered from above. "Just go!"

Without the car, how could we? There was nowhere to hide. All the nearby shops were barren and empty, their windows smashed in and shelving overturned, leaving nothing to conceal us. The infected could overrun them in seconds. Corner us.

Every time the man shouted, "Go!" my heart beat faster. By the time the horde reached us I'd be dead from a heart attack, probably. I didn't know what to do.

Shehan was breathing hard, leaning his head into the car and yelling at the women in a ragged voice. They didn't move an inch. The more we yelled, the more stubbornly they ignored us, and through it all, the sky bucketed down rain on the ruins of Haverhill Road. If I didn't have a heart attack, I might drown.

Shehan grabbed my hand and pulled me away from the car with him. "Forget them, Ciara," he barked, beckoning her forward. "We can't shift those women fast enough. We just have to run for it." He pointed to the nearest side street. We might have been able to make it before the horde arrived, if we could've really run. Shehan wouldn't be able to, though. He'd hardly been capable of walking a few seconds earlier.

"You two go on ahead," he advised, his stare cutting a sharp line between the two of us. "You'll be quicker without me. I'll duck in somewhere. Wait for them to pass and catch up with you."

"No." I shook my head. "We're not going anywhere without you."

He should've known that by now. We were all in this together.

"But you have to find Adam," he reminded me, his eyes swimming in the rain. Somehow they were more golden than I'd ever seen them. I couldn't stop staring.

I glanced at Ciara and knew she was torn. Her first

responsibility was to Adam. But she didn't want to leave Shehan behind any more than I did.

I could hear them coming from around the bend in the road — a collection of ferocious, agonized voices that didn't really sound human any longer. Not like sane humans, anyway. If they were as angry and animal as they sounded, we wouldn't make it out of here. It was too late.

Time slowed. The three of us stood frozen, listening to the sound of our fate. Only for a second, and then we began walking hurriedly again, shoulder to shoulder up Haverhill Road, in the direction of our street. We didn't need to make this easy for the ADS-infected. They'd have to catch up with us first.

The white-haired man rasped at our backs, "Over here! You'll never make it that way."

I ventured a final look over my shoulder at him, expecting to find him in the window. This time the white-haired man stood at street level, in an open doorway next to the hairdressing salon, motioning for us to follow him inside.

We swiveled and jogged towards him, Ciara and me half dragging Shehan with us, making him wince in a way that made me cringe too, only we couldn't afford to slow down. The man calling us forward didn't just have white hair; his face was deeply lined and dotted with age spots. He was at least as old as my grandparents, and as we squeezed into his doorway, jostling Shehan and sending him into louder groans of pain, the man slammed the door behind us with a might that made it shake on its hinges.

I heard the horde flood the street with their animal noises, just on the other side of the wooden door. In the street, metal cracked, wood groaned, and more glass broke. Soon there would be nothing left in the street to damage. Unchecked, the sick would reduce all of Ireland to rubble.

The white-haired man put a finger to his lips, warning us to be quiet. He led us up to his apartment atop the hairdressing salon. The place was cramped but cozy, filled with the most bookshelves I'd ever seen outside of a library or bookstore. A heavy brocade curtain hung across the man's front window, hiding us all from the horde's view. I was fairly sure we'd disappeared through the downstairs door just before the horde had charged around the bend in the road. They might not even notice it in the first place. I hadn't, before the man had appeared there. The exposed hair salon was the thing that stood out. If they *did* take an interest in the door, they could try to break it down, but that wouldn't be a piece of cake — it had a heavy-duty security brace like the kind I'd seen advertised on TV as withstanding over fifteen hundred pounds of force.

"They make an awful racket," the old man complained, turning to bolt into the kitchen. He emerged from it just as swiftly, a surgical mask in one of his veined hands. He slipped the mask over his mouth and then grabbed a walkie-talkie from one of the bookshelves. "I have some young ones with me here," he said into it. "They were out on the street when the horde swept in — I didn't have a choice."

A female voice crackled out from the walkie-talkie. "Seamus, *no*. You must get them out of there. You're taking an awful chance." The woman sounded mortally disap-pointed, like she'd rather the man had left us to the horde.

"I have the mask," he assured her. "Don't you worry, Theresa. I'll be as fit as a fiddle. I'll check in later. Thanks for the warning about the horde, love."

The man we now knew to be Seamus set the walkie-talkie down and stared pensively from one of us to the other. "It could be a while until they've gone," he said. "You may as well make yourself comfortable and tell me your story." Seamus cocked his head to indicate Shehan. "The young fella doesn't look too good."

"I just need to sit awhile," Shehan said, hunching over weakly.

"Stretch out on the sofa there," Seamus instructed, pointing out a maroon loveseat dwarfed by the shelves on either side of it. The couch was the only piece of furniture in the room you could sit on. Aside from a floor lamp, the rest of the space was populated with bookshelves that nearly reached the ceiling. "I'll fetch some chairs for the rest of us."

Ciara and I tried to help Shehan over to the couch, but he shook us off. "*I can do it.* I don't want to be manhandled by you two anymore today, thanks." He shot me a semi-apologetic look as he slipped down into the loveseat, so I'd know he hadn't meant it; he just didn't like feeling vulnerable any better than I did.

"Do you think anything's broken?" I asked him.

"I doubt it. The time I broke my femur it hurt a lot worse than this." Shehan grimaced. "I'll be grand. I just need a couple of minutes."

Soon Seamus was dragging three kitchen chairs into his living room for the rest of us. It wasn't a restful place to be — the din of the ADS-infected wailed through the window as we traded stories. Seamus told us he'd been sick with a bad flu (the regular kind) when ADS struck Ireland. For days he'd been too unwell to leave the apartment, and when he'd begun to feel better, the news had kept him indoors. In the beginning his daughter had dropped off some food at the door for him, but he hadn't heard from her in days and assumed she was sick with ADS too.

"And the woman you spoke to on the walkie-talkie — she isn't sick?" I asked.

Seamus shook his head. "My cousin Theresa was let out of hospital only two weeks ago, after hip surgery. She lives in a flat just around the bend. That's how she was able to warn me about the infected. She's been keeping an eye out. Anyway, she's barely able to make it down the stairs, so she hasn't been outdoors either. Before I took sick with flu I was stopping in to visit and run errands for her every couple of days. The walkie-talkies were a gag gift. I told her I'd be at her beck and call. I never supposed we'd actually need them."

Ciara squeezed her hands in her lap. "So that's why she didn't want you to take us in: she thinks you'll get sick now that we've exposed you to the virus."

"That's right." Seamus adjusted his mask. "But don't you worry about that. I would've had to chance going out sooner or later. What were you lot doing out there yourselves? Searching for supplies?"

"Looking for my little brother." Ciara's voice quavered and then broke. "He had a head start on us. Now he's out there all alone with the infected and the aliens."

"Aliens?" Seamus echoed. "Is it true, then? Theresa says she's seen and heard things in the street, but I supposed she was imagining things from the stress."

"They're real," I said. "We've seen two. One was hurting some of the infected. The other was dead in the street. They make a horrible screeching noise. They're pale gray underneath, but they wear some kind of protective suit, maybe to protect themselves from the sun."

Seamus's thin white eyebrows soared skyward. "I never in my life thought I'd live to hear such things." Ciara began to sniffle.

Seamus's demeanor changed as though someone had flipped a switch. He wagged his finger excitedly at Ciara. "Your brother, was he a young fella?"

"He's nine," Ciara replied, her tone changing. "Have you seen him? He was wearing a Spider-Man hoodie, and he would've been with a big black dog."

"I can't say that I have, but there's a large group of young ones that come poking around every couple of days, scavenging. I've seen them wander back in the direction of Dominic Street more than once, and they always have big dogs or horses with them." Seamus waved his right arm in the direction of the window to show they'd headed east. "They must be staying in a place around the corner there. They might have seen your brother. He could be with them."

My heart leapt. Maybe Adam wasn't as far away as Sutton. Maybe he was within reach and we could still do this — find him and make everything right. As right as it ever could be until there was a cure. We could go home again together.

"Do you think so?" Ciara slid to the edge of her chair. "Have you ever spoken to any of them? What did they look like? Where exactly is this street? Did you see any young kids with them?"

After so many days without speaking to anyone aside from Theresa, Seamus seemed overwhelmed by Ciara's questions. "They're young like you," he replied slowly. "Some a bit older, I'd say. Some a little younger. Dominic Street is just two streets down. That's the direction they come from, and where they always seem to return to."

Ciara jumped up and ran towards the walkie-talkie, pressing it into Seamus's hands. "Ask Theresa if she's seen my brother. *Please*."

Seconds later Theresa confirmed what Seamus had already told us about the other young people he'd seen. "But I haven't noticed a lad in a Spider-Man hoodie," she added, directing her comment at Ciara. "I'm sorry, pet. If I do see him, I'll let your brother know you're searching for him."

"Thank you," Ciara replied, her fingers anxiously brushing her lips. "And … and if you see him, tell him I'm not angry. I just want him to come home."

I grabbed Ciara's free hand, squeezing encouragement into her skin. "We're going to find him. Everything's going to be okay." Outside, the street was teeming with people who no longer remembered their friends and family. Whether they were blissed or bad or blank, their connections to other people were broken. Severed by ADS. Elsewhere, in other countries around the world, scientists were analyzing the virus and working on a cure, but right now it felt as though the thing that mattered most was the four of us being together and safe.

"We have to," Ciara said. "I'm not going back without him." The determination in her eyes underlined her words. "I can't."

"I know." None of us could.

"When you said it wasn't my fault — that's not true," she added. "Adam knows I never wanted him around. Not just since the virus, but always." I heard a fault line opening in Ciara's voice, but she forced herself to continue. "Mom and I were my dad's real family. That's what I used to tell myself. Just us. But it's not true. Adam can be a pest, but I never really try with him." Ciara stared past me. "It should never have been just about how I felt. That's why this happened. So many times I wished he'd disappear. And now that he has all I can think about is finding him."

"We'll get to him," Shehan said, his voice hushed and strong and pained all at once. I stared at him worriedly. He didn't look as though he should be going anywhere in a hurry — more like someone who should spend the next two days in bed.

With Adam possibly only a few blocks away, Ciara kept peeking around the curtain, anxious to move on. Seamus shouted at her to move away from the window every time she did. Hours later, the crowd of infected had thinned by only half and the sky had turned a sleepy shade of gray that meant it would soon be night.

Shehan had fallen asleep on the loveseat with his lower

legs draped over the side. Meanwhile, Ciara and I had shoved our chairs away and settled on the floor, where it was comfier thanks to a thick pile carpet. Seamus kept bringing us cups of tea and plates brimming with sandwich cookies that he probably couldn't spare. He wore gloves as he passed them to us. I hoped the gloves would protect him. It was awful to think we could make him sick.

"Theresa will radio when they've cleared her patch of street," he whispered so as not to wake Shehan. "But it'll only be more dangerous in the dark. You should stay the night here."

"No." Ciara shook her head decisively. "My brother might be miles away already. As soon as the sick disappear we need to go."

With Seamus's mask in place we could only see his eyes. He looked scared for us. He made me think of Granddad somewhere in Dublin and my other grandfather, all the way back in Kingston. They would try to keep us safe if they were here with us. It's what they'd want more than anything.

"You won't be able to help him if you get hurt out there," Seamus pointed out.

We knew that too. "We're all he has now," Ciara whispered. "We have to do whatever we can." Seamus bowed his head, swaying on his feet. "I know you want to think of something to say that will stop us," Ciara continued, "but when the street clears, we have to go."

"*When* it clears," Seamus echoed pointedly. "Let me get you some pillows and blankets in the meantime." He glanced at Shehan's sleeping body. "You should rest too.

Get your strength up for when you go."

Seamus dragged our chairs back to the kitchen. He brought us a pillow and blanket each, then more tea. I didn't even really like tea but slowly began draining my cup. I didn't want to seem ungrateful, and besides, after we left the safety of Seamus's apartment, who knew when we'd next get anything to drink.

"Do you have any paper I could write on?" I asked as Seamus lit a series of candles in the darkening room.

"Reams of it." Seamus smiled, happy to be of help. He retrieved a large pad of blank paper and a ballpoint pen from a drawer under his TV.

"For your journal?" Ciara asked, watching me begin to write.

"*Our* journal," I replied. Because it was the story of the four of us now. It just happened that I was the one telling it.

Ciara nodded dully, draping her blanket around her shoulders and yawning next to me.

So much had happened since I'd written in my journal earlier; I didn't know how I'd ever be able to get it all down on paper. Before long my eyes were heavy. I tried to crank up my speed, my hand practically a blur in front of me. Then I downed more tea, hoping it would keep me awake. Beside me Ciara was out like a light, one arm resting under her head and her knees bent. Turning to Seamus, I was about to ask if he had any coffee. I didn't like the taste of it either, but the caffeine would give me a boost.

Only Seamus was fast asleep, just like Shehan and Ciara. He snored lightly from his wooden chair, oblivious to the threatening noises from outside. I struggled to my feet. They were heavier than my eyelids; they didn't want to budge. Dragging myself to the window, I peeled back the heavy curtain. Two men in their thirties were pushing a shopping cart up the road, a group of others chasing close behind, howling in rage.

I sunk to my knees. Too sleepy to stay upright. Sleepier than I'd ever been in my life. I couldn't control myself. My eyes slapped shut. One of my hands braced itself against the floor. It was the last thing I remembered. Then there was only darkness.

SIXTEEN

DAY TWELVE

CIARA STOOD OVER me, shaking me awake. A dark blue haze leaked through a gap in the curtains, casting Seamus's living room in an eerie half-light. "We need to go!" she shouted. "Morning's coming."

Shehan pushed himself up on the loveseat, staring dazedly over at us. "What happened?"

Ciara glared at Seamus's now empty chair. "He must have drugged us with the tea." But Shehan hadn't drunk any tea; the weakness from his injuries must have kept him asleep through the night.

My mouth felt dry as I scrambled into an upright position. I'd conked out right beside the window, my head nestled against a section of curtain. My mind was still foggy, like it'd been pumped full of clouds.

Ciara and I stared down into the street. We could only see one woman now. She had a muddy face and rain-soaked sundress and stood idly by the mailbox where we thought we'd spotted Adam yesterday. Our car, unfortunately, was toast. Flames engulfed its empty interior. We wouldn't be taking it anywhere ever again.

Footsteps on the wooden floor swung our attention to

Seamus. He'd changed into a fuzzy brown robe and slippers, and he sighed from under his mask as he met our outraged faces. "I'm sorry," he said. "You wouldn't have been safe out there during the night. I couldn't let you go, don't you see?"

"What about my brother?" Ciara cried. "If something happened to him last night I'll never forgive you."

Seamus shuffled closer. "I wouldn't have forgiven myself if I'd allowed you to go out there." He shifted his gaze to Shehan. "How're you feeling, son?"

Shehan frowned heavily at Seamus as he stood. He didn't look any easier on his feet than he had last night, and I frowned too. "We're leaving now," Shehan said.

"Maybe you should wait here," I told him. "Ciara and I will come back for you after."

"What? No!" Shehan's body tilted slightly, his clothes hanging askew on his frame. "You're not going without me. It's too dangerous."

"We're not going far. Just over to Dominic Street to see if Adam's with those other young people." I pointed out the window. "We'll check it out and come back for you before we go to Sutton."

"You can't run," Ciara said bluntly. "You'll slow us down. The car's burnt out, so we'll have to go on foot, and Adam's been on his own too long already."

Shehan's eyes burned with tenacity. "I can make it, Ciara. If we get into a situation where I'm slowing you down and putting you in danger, you two keep going. It's as simple as that."

"Don't be stupid," I insisted. "You should stay here

and get more rest." If something happened to Shehan out there because of the punch he'd taken yesterday I wouldn't be able to forgive myself, just like Seamus wouldn't have forgiven himself for letting us leave last night.

Shehan straightened, not allowing any pain to reach his face. "You don't get to decide for me — either of you. So let's go find Adam. Come on if you're coming." He strode determinedly away from us, briefly pivoting to face Seamus. "Thanks for letting us in. I understand what you did, but you should've let us make up our own minds."

Seamus's head bobbed on his shoulders, but I knew he didn't regret dosing our tea. Not really.

Ciara didn't speak to Seamus on her way out. I nodded goodbye to him and groggily stuffed last night's unfinished journal papers into my pocket. A side of me didn't want to leave the safety of the apartment; the other side was almost as mad at Seamus as Ciara was. But at the last minute I glanced over my shoulder and said, "Take care."

"You too, love," he told me. "Be careful."

Ciara, Shehan, and I trooped downstairs. Seamus locked the door behind us as we stepped back into the outside world. Standing on Haverhill Road, the three of us were as quiet as nighttime stars. The deep blue sky over our heads was cold and unpredictable, like it didn't care what happened to us. I peered up at Seamus's apartment and saw the curtain flutter, then a hand wave slowly.

We turned and began heading in the direction of Dominic Street, our eyes darting around like a crazy person's, searching out the next disaster. The woman in the rain-soaked dress hadn't budged from her spot by the mailbox.

She looked straight through us, scratching at her arm through a wet sleeve.

I trained my eyes on a spot behind the woman, willing her to stay calm. As we hustled past her and down Haverhill Road, Shehan moved faster than he had last night but with obvious stiffness. My body was racked with cold from my still damp clothes, and my nerves were shot. It had stopped raining, at least. I'd have been sick to death of rain, except that these days every drop helped keep us in drinking water.

Adam's name repeated in my head with each step. The three of us were going to find him or go down trying. We'd lost precious hours overnight; we had to make up time. Glass crunched under my feet as I read the nearby street sign: Woodley Lawn. Dominic Street would be next.

Our heads swung to the right to glance down the length of Woodley Lawn. Unlit red brick row houses gaped back at us. Pieces of smashed furniture and ripped-open garbage bags decorated the street. Few cars remained in the driveways, and the ones that were left had been defaced by graffiti and looked as if they'd been attacked with a tire iron. A crow cawed bleakly from a cherry tree. But there wasn't another soul in the street to see. It was as if we were the last three people left on earth.

I peeked back at the woman by the mailbox on Haverhill Road. She'd disappeared now too.

"It's too quiet," Ciara whispered, and she was right. At least when you could hear the infected you knew where they were.

"Quiet's good," Shehan countered. "Quiet is what we

want." We swung right onto Dominic Street. The houses were packed tightly together there too. The same chaotic clutter that seemed to have overtaken most of Dublin spilled out into the middle of Dominic Street — tattered plastic bags, unidentifiable debris, crumpled beer and soft drink cans, and soiled newspapers. Directly ahead of me on the sidewalk, a teddy bear with one eye lay atop a pile of crunched-up juice cartons and a lone tire rim. I stepped around the garbage, my eyes moving between the count- less threateningly dark open doorways.

If Adam were with these other young people, they would be somewhere with a closed door, wouldn't they? Shehan exhaled next to me, like he was thinking the same thing.

"We need to check every house," Ciara said tentatively. "Stand in the open doorways and call Adam's name. Knock at the houses where the doors are locked."

Shehan cleared his throat. "We could stir up trouble that way. Wake the infected."

"But we don't really have a choice, do we?" I asked.

No one answered me. We all knew the answer.

In lockstep we approached the first open doorway. We hovered in its shadows, Ciara gently calling, "Adam? Are you there? Anyone, *anyone*?"

Shehan's stomach growled noisily in response. He'd been asleep when Ciara and I were munching on Seamus's cookies.

We moved on to the next open door, then the one after that. Each time I felt as if I was about to throw up Seamus's cookies and tea. In the third house an open umbrella was spread out on the hallway floor, like someone was waiting for it to dry. Ciara had trouble finding her voice. I was the one who called, "Hello? Is anybody home? Adam? Are you here?"

Next door a dog barked hoarsely. Not Ripley — Ripley's bark was deep.

"The door was closed over there," Shehan noted. "Someone might be home."

We rushed to the next house, Shehan screwing his lips tightly together. He needed to slow down, but we'd barely started looking for Adam.

Ciara rapped quickly at the front door. "We're looking for someone," she said urgently through the wood. "If anyone's in there, please open up. We're harmless. We're just looking for my brother."

The dog's bark creaked like an old rocking chair, more desperate by the second. "It must be all alone in there," I said, sidestepping towards the front window. Inside the house a curtain rustled, a small white dog appearing on top of an armchair. It pawed the window as its eyes drilled into me. "It'll starve!" I cried. "We need to break the window."

Then a pale hand snatched the dog back, yanking the blind closed. "Your brother's not here," the unseen woman shouted back. "Stay away!"

Taken aback, we spun to leave. Ciara was two steps ahead, hurrying on to the next house. Before we could get far, the front door we'd just left behind opened abruptly. The small white dog scooted in our direction. I bent to grab its collar. It yelped and faked me out, swerving left and then right.

"You can have it!" the woman yelled from the rapidly closing door. "It won't shut up." I caught a glimpse of platinum blond hair that hung low into her eyes before the door slammed shut again.

"She must be sick with ADS," Ciara whispered.

The dog whimpered, freezing in the center of the street, not twenty feet ahead of us. Overhead a noise thundered. A flash of bright light slashed through the blue darkness of early morning. The beam snared the dog in its glare, then the rest of us. My head snapped up, my eyes struggling to see past the light in the sky. It was blinding.

My body worked on autopilot. I scurried to snatch the dog up into my arms before it could run again. This time it didn't struggle. The dog shook in my grip, terrified. When I stood, something swooshed past me. A giant, shadowy figure, moving so rapidly it only snagged the corner of my eye.

Dread stood my hair on end. A familiar hand gripped my upper arm. Ciara's shoulder bumped flush against mine, the two of us huddling together under the dazzling light. Then someone — Shehan — grabbed my other arm and pulled us all into a run.

The light seemed endless. Like we'd never be free from it.

But then, somehow, we broke through to the other side. Random pieces of litter gusted past as we slipped away from the glare and back into the ordinary early morning sunshine of Dominic Street.

Ciara extended her arm, pointing at the nearest open doorway. Something pounded against my chest. I wasn't sure whether it was the dog's heart or my own.

We ran into the house without looking back, slamming the door behind us. Shehan tugged the lock into place, quiet descending on us as the shock rattled in our bones.

So close. The thing had been so close to us that I'd felt it. My mind stuttered as I pictured the light from the sky. It had been so powerful that for a minute it had seemed nearly infinite. Not like anything I'd ever seen outside of a movie. Maybe ... maybe not even human.

"It must have been a helicopter," Shehan said doubtfully after a minute, breaking our trance. "A military one, maybe."

"It didn't seem like a helicopter." Ciara's forehead fell into her hands.

Outside the noise died, a creepy silence taking its place.

I rocked the dog in my arms, as much to make myself feel better as for its benefit. "One of the aliens was —" I began, my sentence broken by the dog's leap from my arms. Its claws clacked against the floor as it landed, then skittered down the hallway, disappearing into a room near the back of the house.

"They were looking for it," Ciara said, continuing my half-finished thought as the three of us loitered by the door. "Whatever was in the sky wanted the alien, not us. The alien went right by us — I can't believe it was so close." She shivered, her face crumpling. "How are we ever going to find Adam if we have to keep stopping like this? He could be anywhere by now. There's no sign of any young people around — only that sick woman a few doors down."

"He could still be close," I offered. "Most people who aren't sick are probably staying inside while the thing's out there."

Shehan slumped down in front of the door. "We'll get back out there. We should just give it a few minutes, be as sure as we can that the street's clear."

The dog barked from somewhere we couldn't see. Three quick yelps that sounded like *help, help, help.*

Somebody stumbled towards us in the hallway. In the darkness it was hard to make out his or her face. I reached behind me to unlock the door. Shehan struggled to his feet.

"Sorry," Ciara said breathlessly. "We thought the house was empty."

"It's okay. It's okay." The guy smiled as he stepped into clearer view. His voice was calm — happy, even — and he didn't look a day older than twenty-two. Stubble dotted his pale cheeks and chin, and the lettering across the chest of his T-shirt said: DON'T GROW UP. IT'S A TRAP. "I'm glad you're here. It's been dead boring on my own. But I think ... I think I'm starting to remember now."

Ciara and I traded hopeful looks. Could people recover from the virus the same way everyone recovers from the common cold? Since people in their twenties were the last ones to get the virus, it was possible they'd be first to get better too.

The guy jogged closer. "I know you, don't I? The lot of you. We were" — he tapped his forehead — "was it school? We were all in school together?"

I watched Ciara munch her lip. There was no way she

or Shehan had ever gone to school with this guy; he was too much older than them.

"It doesn't matter, doesn't matter." He swatted the air, grin swelling. "Sit down. You three look dead tense."

He should've been tense too, considering everything that had happened lately.

"We can't stay long," Ciara told him. "We're looking for my brother, but one of the aliens was outside in the street and something was looking for it."

"Sure." The guy kept nodding, like talking about aliens roaming the street was the most normal thing in the world. In the distance, the dog whined.

"Have you seen a little boy with a dog?" I asked.

"I don't think so." He scratched his chin. "What did they look like?" Before any of us could offer a description, the guy opened his mouth wide. "Hey, I know you lot! I think I'm starting to remember."

I fought a frown. Even if he *had* seen Adam he'd probably forgotten. He wasn't getting any better, that was for sure. He was looping.

"It's okay," the guy told me. "Don't worry. I won't stay if you don't want me to. I didn't mean to bother you."

Shehan glanced at me from the corner of his eyes while the guy continued to stare at us expectantly. "Sit down," Shehan said casually, motioning for the guy to move into the closest room. "Make yourself at home."

Ciara and I played along, pretending we were the ones who belonged here and that the guy with the stubble was the visitor. There was no point in explaining otherwise.

The guy went first, ambling in the direction Shehan

had indicated. The three of us followed, sticking as close together as was humanly possible. Then the dog dashed into our midst, yapping at our feet. Shehan tripped over it, falling into the living room entranceway and knocking the side of his skull hard.

Legs buckling, he went down in a flash. Ciara and I squatted beside him, the dog whimpering and sprinting back in the direction it had come from.

"Say something," I prompted worriedly. "Are you all right?"

"Another knock like that and I won't need blackout flu to forget who I am," Shehan kidded, his words spilling out at half their usual speed. Ciara and I reached for his hands, pulling him up carefully. It visibly strained Shehan to rise to his feet, and again I found myself wishing he'd stayed with Seamus.

As we inched into the living room, the flooring beneath our feet vibrated. Noise pounded through the walls, light stronger than sunshine bursting through the window blind. I ducked instinctively, pulse racing. Whatever had been in the sky a few minutes ago was back with a vengeance.

The three of us squished fearfully onto a worn beige couch. Across from us, the guy in the T-shirt dropped into a matching armchair. He clamped his hands over his ears and stared at us quizzically.

It was then I noticed the marks on his wrists. Fresh rope burns. Not long ago someone had tied his arms.

Ciara bit her nails beside me. Shehan hunched over and wound his hands around the back of his neck. My molars clacked together repeatedly. *Clink. Clink.* When you get that scared, you can't really think. You just exist, breathing and breathing and somehow leaping from one moment to the next. The panic had hit me so many times since the epidemic first struck that I was starting to forget what normal felt like.

The noise outside blared on and on, freezing us in a state of high alert. For minutes at a time, I didn't do anything but listen, inhale, and exhale. Then my fingers found their way into my pocket to pull out my unfinished journal notes from Seamus's apartment. I'd taken his pen, too, and my fingers closed spontaneously around it — like they knew what was good for me even if I didn't — picking up where I'd left off.

The steady motion of my fingers around the pen kept me from all-out panicking. Before this summer I'd never had any interest in keeping a journal, but now it felt like glue. My friends, the journal, and thought of seeing my mom and dad again were the things holding me together.

The blasts of light and sound went on for so long that my right thumb went numb, but I didn't stop writing. Not until the guy jumped out of his chair without warning, stalking agitatedly towards the front door. "Don't go out there!" we shouted, rushing after him. Ciara clawed at the back of his T-shirt, trying to stop him.

He never turned back. Unlocking the door, he sprang into the unknown, disappearing into a blazing, vivid wall of light.

We shrank away from it, my heart in my throat. A second noise streamed into the first. Something I didn't want to hear and would never forget. A long, harrowing squeal that sounded like the stuff of nightmares.

SEVENTEEN

CIARA AND I slammed the door shut behind the guy, yanking the lock back into place. Shehan rubbed his jaw, his face stretched long with guilt. Mine was long too; I could almost feel it scrape against the floor. But we couldn't take the risk of going after the guy to drag him back inside. If something happened to us, there would be no one left to search for Adam.

Together, we moved slowly away from the door, settling ourselves deeper in the hallway. I half-waited for a knock — the guy changing his mind and wanting back in. If he *had* rapped at the door, we might not have heard it above the thundering from outside anyway. It sounded like the world was ending, being torn apart by the seams.

We didn't dare move, not even to hide deeper in the house. The three of us sat shoulder to shoulder on the wooden floor. Minutes passed. Hours. I gripped the journal pages between my forefinger and thumb, like rosary beads.

My past felt like eons ago. I felt different. Like the present had expanded, taking up all the room inside me. But I could remember the old Naomi well, and I wrote out a list for her.

THINGS THAT USED TO SCARE ME

- Spiders — the longer the legs, the scarier they seemed. In Australia, where they have big *and* hairy spiders, I would never have been able to shut my eyes without checking every nook and cranny of a bedroom.
- Giving speeches — I never minded when people watched me play hockey, but I used to hate the way the whole class stared when students were giving a speech, like they were waiting for you to make a mistake ... which they probably weren't, but it felt that way.
- Great white sharks — I've only seen them up close in movies, but they looked terrifying. Those cold dark eyes and crazy teeth.
- Serial killers — they can look and seem normal, which was one of the scariest things about them.
- Death (my own and other people's) — who isn't scared of that?

And then I made a list for the person I was now.

THINGS THAT SCARE ME

- Death.
- When there's no emergency number to call anymore.
- Unexplainable loud noises.
- Blinding lights.
- Knowing I can make people sick.
- Seeing things that should be impossible, but aren't. Things that want to hurt you.
- Losing people who are still alive, somewhere.
- Giving up.

- If ADS lasts long enough for me to grow up: forgetting!

Sometimes there were short breaks in the noise, quiet breaking through. Sometimes the light dimmed too. Once we heard shouting from the street. Frightened human shouting.

Through it all, the small white dog we'd brought inside with us was oddly absent and silent. If Ripley had been with us she'd have stayed close to watch over us. Not this dog. It must have been cowering in a corner of the house somewhere.

Finally, during another outbreak of near-silence, Shehan murmured, "I need water. I'm going to check out the kitchen — see if there's anything left to drink."

Ciara and I stood up to go with him. No one wanted to be left behind.

Walking into the kitchen, my eyes zoomed to the open refrigerator. A package of funky-looking cold cuts rotted next to a container of what must have been room-temperature mayonnaise. Ciara froze next to me, her cheeks as gray as ash. My gaze followed her stare, over the top of the fridge door and towards the sliding door at the other end of the kitchen.

The small white dog sat anxiously at the foot of the sliding door. Its eyes burned a hole in the spot in front of it, its attention rapt. My gaze froze when I saw what the dog was looking at, my eyelids forgetting to blink. I lost my breath, my pupils dilating. A sliding door was the only thing separating us and the dog from a pair of towering aliens. In the backyard, not fifteen feet from where we stood, the aliens vibrated so quickly that I thought of insects. Their black second-skin covering hid their large faces. But they could see us. Everything inside me told me so. Sickness rolled through my stomach, my eyes watering.

The glass sliding door began to shake. My dread mushroomed. The aliens' legs blurred underneath them, the tremor increasing. Earlier this year, Mr. Nishiada had told my class that scientists in Japan had created unbreakable glass as strong as steel. In the future, windows and sliding doors could offer us some real protection. But the three of us didn't have long. Soon the sliding door glass would shatter under the strain. It quivered as if in the middle of an earthquake. My fingers shook along with it, the vibration from the aliens like a weird ghostly hum in the back of my throat.

"Let's go," I whispered, sliding one of my feet gingerly backwards. "Slowly."

No sudden movements. That's what my instinct said. If we ran, the aliens would chase.

Ciara and Shehan slid back along with me, the three of us nearly skating. Smooth. Steady. Scared to death. Our hearts vibrating on the frequency of fear.

I turned as soon as we were clear of the kitchen, the hall hiding us from the aliens' view. My feet darted for the door, Shehan and Ciara hot on my heels. Together we burst out into Dominic Street. My shoulder and a sliver of my face caught a splinter of light from whatever hung in the sky. I didn't twist to look at it. I tore in the opposite direction — moving farther along Dominic Street with every step.

Scattered light danced on my back. Shehan and Ciara sprinted next to me, their faces blurred by speed and glare. Something moved in the distance up ahead. As we left the glow of light behind the figures came into focus — two girls on a motorcycle, long red hair spooling out behind the one who sat in back.

The motorcycle rounded the corner, zooming onto a wide cross street. We ran after it, turning left. We scanned the horizon, but there was no sign of the girls by the time we got to the next street.

"Which way?" Shehan had to shout so we could hear him above the noise from Dominic Street.

Ciara pointed to the next right. It was a shot in the dark — a fifty-fifty chance. Our legs carried us right, Shehan beginning to slow as we squeezed between a pair of parked cars with their gas tank doors hanging open. In the ordinary sunlight, Shehan's forehead gleamed with sweat. I slowed along with him, even if it meant losing the motorcycle.

Ciara pulled ahead, her feet practically flying. She slowed to holler back to us, "I see them!" Waving wildly, she called to the girls, "Stop! Stop! We need to talk to you."

Ciara sped forward again, leaving us in the dust. We saw her lurch up a driveway where one of the girls vaulted forward, leaping onto a guy's back and wrestling him to the ground. I caught a glimpse of his T-shirt as he twisted and fell: DON'T GROW UP. IT'S A TRAP. It was him! The guy who'd fled the house. Except for being tackled, he was all right. Still in one piece.

The second girl flipped out the motorcycle's kickstand

with her right foot, rushing towards the fight. Together, the girls forced the guy onto his chest and quickly bound his hands behind his back.

"What're you doing to him?" Ciara demanded, catching up to them.

Their heads snapped up to look at her, the red-haired girl digging her knee into the guy's spine. "Not that it's any of your business, but he's our friend. We're just trying to keep him safe."

"We can't stay out here long!" I hollered, looking over my shoulder at the halo of light from Dominic Street.

The second girl wore a green anorak, spattered with mud. "She's right," she said. "We all need to get inside — we don't know what those ships want. One of them looked as if it might be a human craft, but the other one moved so strangely — no way it's earthly."

"Just wait," Ciara pleaded. "I need to know if you've seen my little brother. Someone said there was a group of young people over this way that might have seen him."

"He was with a big black dog," I added. "He's nine years old."

The redhead pulled the guy up into a seated position as she replied, "I know someone who saw him. He said the kid wouldn't speak to him except to say he didn't talk to strangers — then the boy sped off on his bike."

"And you all just let him go? A little kid alone like that?" Ciara glowered at the girls with an outrage that could power half of Dublin. Both girls looked anywhere from eighteen to twenty-one, but as they stared back at her something in their eyes seemed older. Maybe our eyes had it too.

"Look, we're packed to the gills where we're staying," the girl replied. "We can't chase down everyone we see and take them in. But if it helps, my friend saw a hand-bill in your brother's fist — the one the government posted all over the area instructing kids with no one left to look after them to go to Haverhill Heights Comprehensive School."

"Where's the school?" I asked.

"Not far. On Rathvale Heights, just around the corner from Haverhill Road. You won't be able to miss it."

From his spot sandwiched between the two girls, the guy let perfect white teeth peek out from under his top lip in the beginnings of a smile. "Hey, don't I know you?" he said, staring cheerfully up at Ciara, Shehan, and me. "I think I'm starting to remember."

"Hello again," I said, as if maybe we really had gone to school together. "See you later, maybe?"

The guy nodded placidly, his sea-blue eyes younger and less troubled than his friends'. "After a while, crocodile," he replied, and for a moment I felt like I could breathe again. Adam wasn't with the group Seamus had seen, but he could still be close. Much nearer than Sutton.

An abrupt boom shot into our ears from several streets away. *Dominic Street.* The sky danced with light. The three of us turned as one, sprinting in the opposite direction — leaving the furious sound and blaze in our wake. Shehan quickly fell behind. Even with the hours and hours of rest we'd had back at the house on Dominic Street, he was wearing down like an old windup clock.

"We can't take shelter again," Ciara cried as we hurtled

forward. "We need to keep going. Adam's been on his own too long already."

"I know." I glanced uneasily back at Shehan. "If we keep heading south, we should be able to stay clear of the ships. Then cut left back towards Haverhill Road."

Ciara turned to check on Shehan too. "I'm okay," he insisted. "I've just got a stitch. Don't give me that pitying stare — I could still beat either of you in a race if I needed to."

Ciara rolled her eyes like she would've on any number of summer days before ADS hit, but when her eyes flicked back to mine they were crowded with equal parts worry and determination. Then Shehan sped forward, passing us, careful not to look at either of us.

We thought of Adam. Adam, with only Ripley for company. Adam, waiting for us, although he didn't know we were coming. *We're on our way, Adam*, I said in my mind. *Hang in there*. And for a time, not one of us slowed down.

EIGHTEEN

HAVERHILL ROAD WAS unoccupied except for a rangy cat with a patch of fur missing from its back. From the main road, Dominic Street's noise was threatening but not deafening. The light in the sky over in that direction resembled an approaching thunderstorm. I tried not to think about the aliens and the ships. Not to think, period. Panic wants you to run, and our bodies were already obeying. There was nothing else we could do. We had to keep going.

Veering left onto Rathvale Heights, Shehan paused to catch his breath. Ciara and I stopped with him, neither of us mentioning that he should've waited with Seamus. When we started walking again we weren't as swift, but we could already see the school ahead on our right, two school buses covered in spidery black graffiti parked diagonally in the middle of the street, one behind the other.

There were so many old buildings in Ireland that I'd figured the school would be ancient too. It wasn't. With its light brickwork and large, airy windows, Haverhill Heights looked more like a modern office building. Some of the ground-floor windows were broken and had been boarded up; each of the intact windows was secured with wooden panels too. Other than that, the school seemed to be in one piece, and Ciara started running ahead of us, shouting Adam's name.

Shehan and I followed at a more restrained pace, watching Ciara veer towards the front door of the school as we neared the first bus. A drop of rain clipped the end of my nose. From this distance, the school looked terminally quiet, no one in sight. But that didn't mean anything. It was only smart to make a place look empty if you didn't want to be discovered there.

Another drop landed on my lips and cascaded down my chin, my skin prickling up for no good reason. *There's no horde, no aliens, and no strange ships,* I told myself. *Just a little rain. Relax and breathe.*

Shehan reached for my hand, sensing my anxiety. Fingers laced, we continued forward.

Then something whizzed by us, so close that it skimmed my leg. I heard it bark as it sped past us, a black wolf body spurting towards Ciara.

"Ripley!" I shouted, Ciara spinning to look at her.

My eyes scanned the street, expecting to find Adam at any second. Surely he couldn't be far. But Ripley kept charging onward alone, beyond Ciara, away from the school and down the street.

"Stop, Ripley!" Ciara hollered. "Ripley! Ripley, come here, girl!" She turned to chase after her, leaving Shehan and I to pick up the pace and follow them.

But there was no time for that. In the next moment, a familiar chirp sent my free hand flying to my right ear. The aliens were nearby too. Not just one or two of them. *Many.* I tightened my grip on Shehan's hand as I gaped at them just beyond the school. Five of the creatures hovered in the street, dark and foreboding. Their large heads bent together so that they were touching, their long bodies shuddering like someone being electrified.

The things separated us from Ciara and Ripley. In the distance, I could see Ciara darting farther and farther away. I opened my mouth to call for her, clamping it shut again just as quickly. My arms were shaking and my breath was snatched up by the chilling sight and sound of the aliens, their black covering torn in spots to reveal their eerie pale gray skin.

Shehan and I could never make it to the school now. The things were too close to it. We couldn't reach Ciara either. And Shehan was worn to the bone after running through the pain of his injuries too many times already. A quick getaway was impossible. We were stuck.

I glanced at the bus next to us. We were ten feet from its accordion-like front door, but a padlock was fastened around the bottom of it.

I swung around, pulling Shehan with me and doubling back to the rear of the bus. I'd seen a boy do this on a dare at a field trip once — break into a school bus through the back window. It hadn't been difficult. "We need to pull the levers down," I cried, thankful we were both tall enough to reach for them. I grabbed the left lever at the bottom of the window while Shehan yanked down the right. As I leapt onto the bumper, the alien screech assaulted my ears.

Were they coming for us? I didn't know. I tugged furiously at the back window, pulling it open it until it caught and held. "Shehan!" I turned to make sure he was still with me. He was standing on the bumper too, ready to squeeze himself through the window right behind me. Shimmying inside, I grabbed for the row of seats in front of me to steady myself. Shehan landed next to me, his fingers splayed out on the sticky bus floor, pushing himself upward with a groan I could see instead of hear. We slid into the back row of the bus together, hunching down into the fabric like we were chameleons who could hide ourselves from predators.

My hands clamped themselves to my ears, blocking out as much of the noise as I could. Shehan's hands protected his ears too, his eyes glimmering with pain. Was this how things ended after all we'd been through? The four of us divided — Shehan and I like bugs caught in a spiderweb?

Ciara, I mouthed, as I stared into Shehan's pupils. She was out there on her own. If things were going to end this way, at least the three of us should've been together.

Shehan nodded, seeming to grasp what I meant. Then his lips parted and formed what looked like, *She'll be okay*.

He had no way of knowing that, but I nodded and mouthed the words *Find her after* back to him. Because what else were we supposed to do except hold on and believe that she'd somehow be able to get away from the things?

Maybe it was minutes or maybe hours — I was so scared that I couldn't keep track of time — all I know is that the things screeched on and on, the hostile sound seeming ever louder until I couldn't stand it anymore and pushed past Shehan and into the aisle, him grabbing for my hand to hold me back.

I shook him off, trying to calm him with my eyes. Hunching low I crept to the front of the bus and peered out the window. A hulking clump of alien bodies — between fifteen and twenty of them now — twitched and jerked, their bowed heads pressing together wherever possible and their mechanical howl repeatedly cresting and descending.

One of them broke apart from the group to stare in my direction, my hands slipping from my ears for an instant. It wasn't near enough that I could make out its eyes, but I gasped as it looked at me. I stumbled back, the terror knotting into my calves and spine.

Somehow my jelly-like legs still worked. They dashed me back to Shehan, my face as stiff as a new sheet of poster board.

What? he mouthed.

So many. I threw my hands apart to illustrate their numbers and slid into the seat next to him, our legs pressing together. At first I thought the vibration was coming from us — nerves making us tremble. Suddenly the sensation was everywhere, first like an earthquake and then like a wave washing the bus out to sea. The things were closing around the bus, lifting it into the air as they surrounded it.

This was it. Would they kill us or take us prisoner? I tore my left hand from my ear, throwing my right arm over my head so my armpit could block one ear while my right hand blocked the other. Meanwhile, my left hand reached for Shehan's. We clutched each other's fingers so tightly that I'm surprised the bones didn't snap, the school bus shaking and a cloud of unearthly noises storming around us.

I closed my eyes and thought of my dad. Would he ever find out what had happened to me? My mind sprang back to the summer days years ago when he and Mom had taught me to ride a bike without training wheels. They'd taken turns holding on to the back of my bicycle while the other one jogged next to me calling encouragement. Afterwards we'd headed home and had a scoop each of whatever flavor my dad had concocted with the ice cream maker.

Mom's absolute favorite was always cherry. The flavor zinged between my teeth as her image filled my head. Would ADS end someday and my mom be restored to her usual self? She and dad reunited? I hoped so. I wanted that for them so much that it seemed to stop time.

That's not possible, I know. Time never stops. But that was how it felt. Like a paused second in time. And then … bit by bit the moment began to ease and pass. My heart was still beating, my lungs sucking in oxygen and expelling carbon dioxide. The noise and vibrations dulled and receded, Shehan's grip on my fingers as steady as ever.

It was minutes, I think, before I opened my eyes again. Was I waking up dead?

My eyelashes fluttered, my vision focusing on Shehan's sturdy fingers, and then his hair where it was shaved at the sides. His eyes were still shut, his face creased with what looked like a blend of panic and the pain he must've caused himself squeezing through the bus window after his injuries.

We weren't dead. Somehow the things had decided to let us live and had left us in peace.

I didn't know why, but I knew what we had to do next.

"I think they're gone," I whispered, my voice a silent ghost to my ears. I rubbed my thumb against the side of Shehan's finger and raised my voice. "You can open your eyes now. We're safe."

It was time for us to go find Ciara and Adam.

NINETEEN

THERE REALLY WASN'T any such thing as safe anymore. Not for more than a few minutes at a time. But we were still breathing, still free, and I tapped my foot against Shehan's, waiting for him to join in my relief.

"Shehan, hey." It was like someone had stuffed my ears with cotton balls; I could barely hear myself. "Come on!" My throat strained with effort as I tried to provoke a reaction, but he was as relaxed and unmoving as if he were sleeping.

No one could have fallen asleep with the aliens shrieking and shaking the bus like it was the end of the world. It could've been hitting his head on the doorway earlier, combined with yesterday's injuries, that had done this to him. Shehan was out cold.

I pressed my palm to his cheek and then gripped his thigh, trying to force him back into consciousness. Shehan didn't even flinch, but the rise and fall of his chest told me he was still breathing. I began to shake him, my hands on his shoulders as I shouted my lungs out. It was the last thing I should've been doing — I should've remembered that from all my years of hockey. The coach and his assistants made sure we all knew the rules about dealing with player injuries. *Don't slap, shake, or throw water on someone who's fainted or lost consciousness*. The knowledge bounded back to me as I stared at Shehan's motionless eyelashes.

Desperate, I jumped to my feet and paced the aisle, my eyes scouring the bus for anything that might help. The only thing left behind was a beaten-up knapsack squatting in the third row. I snatched the bag up and unbuckled it, my hands diving inside and grasping at the contents: a blue plastic comb, a notebook with a torn cover and a tiny dull pencil tangled within its wire binding, an emptied-out wallet, a half-eaten chocolate bar, tangled earbuds, and a mascara tube.

Useless.

I flung the knapsack down and hurried back to Shehan. Crouching in front of him, I grabbed his kneecaps and pleaded with him to wake up until I was hoarse. Shehan stayed as still as a statue.

I stifled the cry rising in my chest — there was no time for that — I needed to find him help. Carefully, I eased Shehan's head and chest down so that the bottom of the seat cushioned his head. No one would be able to see him from outside the bus that way. Hopefully they'd think it was abandoned and keep moving.

I ran for the knapsack again, scribbled down a note, and slid it directly under Shehan's head:

I couldn't wake you up! Going for help. Wait for me here if you wake up so that we don't lose each other.

Naomi

I squeezed myself out the back window, shutting it behind me. Yesterday morning there'd been four of us, and now I was almost alone. Something began to crumble inside me at the thought.

In a few hours it would be dark, the streets even less safe than they were right now. But with the aliens gone, the school was within reach. Adam would be there, wouldn't he? Ripley's presence outside must have been proof of that. And if the school was a sanctuary for kids set up by the government, someone might know how to find medical help. No one could cure ADS yet, but there had to be people somewhere who knew something about treating a concussion.

I scrambled towards the school like I was being chased. Two sets of glass doors marked the entrance, a collection of solid wooden cabinets pressed up against them from the inside so that I couldn't see past them. My hand rapped briskly at the glass, my non-functioning ears straining to hear any reaction from inside.

I banged harder at the doors, my foot kicking at them impatiently too. "Hello!" I called. "Can you hear me? I have someone out here who needs help. Adam, are you in there? It's Naomi. Please open the door!"

Had we wasted our time coming to the school? Just because the girl on the motorcycle knew someone who'd spied Adam with a handbill didn't mean he was here. He and Ripley could've gotten separated. *Please please please*, I chanted inside my head. *Someone answer, someone help me.*

No one answered and no one came.

I took off running again, my legs carrying me to the spot where I'd last seen Ciara chasing after Ripley. The rest of Rathvale Heights was lined with semi-detached houses. Front gardens that had probably once been well tended were in shambles, litter strewn across them and many of the flowers and small shrubs trampled. The same spidery graffiti plastered across the school buses defaced a few of the houses.

My head jerked left and right, hoping for a glimpse of Ciara or her dog. Part of me was afraid I'd stumble across their bodies. Another part was worried that I'd never see either of them again.

Then I felt something knock against my back. I jumped in fear, expecting to have to fight off one of the infected. Instead a sweet but muffled sound met my ears. *Ripley*. She careened in front of me, her paws reaching for me as she bounded up joyfully, greeting me with her bark.

Arms reached for me next, flinging themselves around my neck and hugging me close. A strand of Ciara's hair scrunched into my cheek as I hugged her back, snotty and starting to blubber because I'd thought maybe I'd lost her for good.

"You got away!" I cried, my eyes emptying out. "They didn't hurt you."

"What?" Ciara mouthed. Then I realized she wasn't mouthing the word but saying it out loud. It was just that neither of us could hear properly since the alien encounter.

"You're alive!" I shouted.

"I grabbed Ripley and hid in the house back there!" Ciara hollered, pointing to an open doorway behind us.

"The noise spooked her like I've never seen." Ciara's eyes had begun to leak too. "I didn't know what happened to you. I was so scared that —" She stopped short. "Where's Shehan? Why isn't he with you?"

"He passed out on the bus," I yelled. "I can't get him to wake up. We need to get him help."

"Do you think he's in a coma?" she asked fearfully.

"I don't know." I shook my head, my desperation kept in check by Ciara's presence. We jogged back in the direction of the bus together, Ripley galloping between us.

We arrived just in time to see one of the school's front doors inch cautiously open. I barely had time to register the sight when Ripley turned and scampered for the door. Suddenly it was thrown open wide, revealing four people standing on the other side of the threshold — two scrawny twin girls roughly ten or eleven years old, a cheerful-looking middle-aged woman in a stained apron, and Adam Kavanagh himself, minus his Spider-Man hoodie and now holding tight to Ripley's collar.

Behind them, the hallway was empty except for the wooden cabinets that had been blocking the door previously. What had happened to all the other ADS orphans who were supposed to be gathered at the school, I had no idea, but as I watched Ciara scamper to the door and throw her arms around her brother, I felt as if we'd leapt a step closer to saving ourselves. *We'd found Adam*. He was safe and sound, and we'd never be separated again. My eyes filled themselves up with him second after second, like I could never get enough of his nine-year-old face.

I gave Adam and Ciara a few seconds to themselves,

then I ran to join them, hugging Adam hard. He pretended the hug was only something to endure, but leaned into me as I went to pull away. "Didn't you hear me knocking and calling for you?" I asked.

I couldn't make out his reply, and Ciara, whose ears were less affected by the aliens than mine were — probably because she'd been able to get farther away — repeated it, "They shut themselves up in a storage room near the back, cutting themselves off from the alien noise as much as they could."

"We're so glad we found you," Ciara said to her brother, loudly enough for me to hear. "But we have to help Shehan now. He won't wake up. Is there a doctor here?" Ciara pointed to the smiling middle-aged woman. "Is she in charge?"

"She's infected," one of the twin girls shouted. "But she's been really good to us, watching over us as much as she can, even though she doesn't remember anything. We didn't want to go with all the other kids when they took them to Wicklow, and she helped us hide."

"The three of them are the only ones left here," Adam added. He started to explain about the handbill that had led him here.

"There's no time to talk about that now." I pointed at the bus. "We need to help Shehan. The doors are padlocked. We'll have to climb back in through the window."

"Take him," Adam said to the girls as he motioned to Ripley. One of them looped her fingers through Ripley's collar. The twins, Ripley, and the kindly blissed woman withdrew back into the school while the three of us headed for the bus. I climbed in first, Ciara giving Adam a boost. I pulled him into the bus with me and then helped Ciara inside.

Shehan was just as I'd left him, the note crammed under his head. Ciara skimmed his hand with her fingers, frowning. "What do we do?" She looked back at me.

I could remember a little more about fainting and concussions now. *Don't leave an unconscious person alone.* I'd gotten that wrong too. *Don't move them unnecessarily. Don't give them anything to drink.*

There were a lot of *don'ts*, but most of the *dos* involved calling for help. That and making sure the airway was clear. At least Shehan was breathing just fine. I could see the rhythmic rise and fall of his chest.

But now there were no emergency numbers to call. No open hospitals or medical clinics, except for the ones dealing with ADs, and those didn't sound safe anymore. We could split up again — one of us could go look for whatever kind of medical people might still be left while the other stayed here with Shehan and Adam. But once the four of us divided again there was always the chance we wouldn't come back together. We'd faced so many risks outside already. It was practically a miracle that the four of us had found each other again.

Ciara stared at me uncertainly. "How long has he been like this?" she asked.

"Since the aliens left." People with concussions were supposed to rest. Shehan had mostly done the opposite, and what I was about to say was a risk in itself, but I didn't know what else to do or where to take him. "At least one of us needs to stay with him and make sure he keeps breathing, but it's starting to get late in the day. What do you think if we waited until morning to see if he wakes up on his own?"

"What if he doesn't?" Adam said, his eyes reddening. "What if what the aliens did to him makes it so he can't ever wake up?"

"It wasn't the aliens." My tone aimed for calm. "Just a person. Someone punched him in the stomach earlier and he fell."

"One of the infected in the streets?" Adam cried, more upset by the moment. "That means it's my fault he's hurt because you all came out to look for me."

"No," Ciara insisted, her hand reaching for Adam's shoulder. "It's not. It's this stupid virus that has blacked out everyone's memories — a microscopic parasite. That's whose fault this is. And Shehan's going to be okay, you'll see."

Ciara's eyes met mine over the top of Adam's head. *Won't he*, her eyes seemed to ask. Mine were asking the exact same question. One neither of us knew the answer to.

"Like you said," Ciara began firmly, "we'll wait awhile for him to wake up. It could be that he just needs sleep to heal. And maybe it's better to spend the night here anyway. None of us should be out in the streets when it gets dark."

"Stay in the bus?" Adam asked, wide-eyed.

"Yeah," Ciara and I replied at the same time.

"Except for the graffiti, it looks like it's been left alone so far," I added. "And it's locked. We can take turns watching Shehan and looking out for whatever else might come by."

The aliens might return, or another horde might stampede through the streets, trampling everything and everyone in its path. But that was a chance we could take together. Give ourselves one night before we'd have to break up the group again.

Ciara and Adam sat in the seat across from Shehan, and I sat in the seat directly in front of him, each of us hunching low so we couldn't easily be spotted from outside the bus. I pulled what was left of the chocolate bar from the knapsack and broke it into three. Ciara's stomach grumbled as she swallowed her chunk, a growly wild animal sound that almost made Adam smile.

"They have lots of food in the school," he told us. "Even more than we have at Shehan's house. They showed me. Enough tinned chili and curry to last forever."

"Maybe we should ask the three of them to come back with us tomorrow," Ciara said. "After Shehan wakes up." I could see what she was doing by planning for tomorrow — trying to be positive for Adam's sake — and I joined in.

"We should ask Daniel and Anish too." I wiped my chocolaty fingers on my jeans. "Maybe they could move in next door with the little girl they found." The idea made sense. Safety in numbers. It didn't just have to be something to say to stop Adam from being scared. We could really do it, just like the young people in the vicinity of Dominic Street had. "Or if Daniel and Anish don't want to relocate, we could move in next to them. Pool our resources."

My grandparents' street would be better — farther away from the main road, where less infected could happen by. The main thing is that living close together would be good for everyone, and the three of us talked the plan over as the somber sky dimmed to starless black: how so many pairs of hands would make the move easy; how having a larger group around would mean someone could always keep watch over the street. We even, as we got a little giddy about the possibilities, debated what was better, canned chili or canned curry.

Through it all we watched over Shehan, staring at him breathe. It was harder to see in the dark, and from time to time I'd reach over the seat back and stick my hand in front of his mouth to feel the warmth of his breath. My mind kept saying the same things over and over while I looked at him. *Hang on, Shehan. Wake up and come back to us.*

When it was time to sleep I took first watch, waking Ciara when I couldn't keep my eyes open anymore. Being in the bus in the blackness was more frightening than it had been during the day, but I was exhausted from everything we'd been through.

In the darkness I dreamt about us and all our moms and dads — healthy the way they used to be — my dad baking everyone manicotti in an outdoor oven powered by the sun. Even Shehan's mom was there, wearing a long floral dress and a wide-brimmed sun hat and smelling like lilies and mint leaves. The rectangular wooden table we were about to eat from was positioned in the middle of a green field flecked with wildflowers. The sky was the same dazzling blue-green color as a tropical ocean, and as my mom smiled at me and handed over a plate, I was happier than I'd ever been. Happy the way you can be when you don't have any idea how many things can go wrong, how many things there are to be afraid of, and how many people you might lose.

DAY THIRTEEN

I didn't want to leave that happiness and wake up yet, and maybe I would've kept my eyes closed longer and eaten up my dad's pretend manicotti, only then I felt something soft on my cheek. As I opened my lashes to real life, Shehan smiled down at me in the pale morning light. He was holding the note I'd written him, and he said, "We didn't lose each other." Then he glanced over at the seat across from his, where Ciara and Adam were sleeping with their heads propped together. "You found them." He rubbed both his ears roughly, suddenly perplexed. "Hey, I think I've gone partially deaf."

"It won't last," I replied loudly. I could already hear better than when I'd fallen asleep. I pulled myself up in my seat and kissed Shehan quickly on the lips, nearly as bursting with joy as I'd been in my sleep. "You scared us yesterday." Kind of an understatement.

"Sorry," he shouted, Ciara and Adam beginning to stir from the noise. "I feel much better now."

Me too.

I still didn't know what was going to happen to us, four kids surrounded by aliens and millions of ADS-infected, but staring into Shehan's eyes, with Ciara and Adam struggling into wakefulness in my peripheral vision, I was full of hope. We were together again. Not like in my dream, but as close to it as was possible in the here and now.

We would find a way to survive. And when we got back to Sykes Close, I would write the rest of our story down. Day by day by day. For the four of us, mostly. But for whoever else might want to read it, too.

I grabbed Shehan's hand and fit my fingers between his. "We made a plan last night," I announced, a grin digging into my face. "I think you'll like it. It starts with going home."

ACKNOWLEDGEMENTS

Stricken wouldn't be complete without saying thanks to the people who made this book possible. As always, endless gratitude goes to Barry Jowett for his patience and for his sage editorial guidance. Both are much appreciated!

Thank you to Stephanie Thwaites and Sara Crowe for insightful early notes on the manuscript.

Nick Craine, you've given me the best book cover I've ever had. I can't thank you enough.

Thank you to book designer Tannice Goddard and copy-editor Andrea Waters for their wonderful work on *Stricken*. You make me look and sound good.

Thank you, also, to Bryan J. Ibeas and Marc Côté for Cormorant's continued support.

Finally, thanks, Paddy, for being as fascinated by things that go bump in the night as I am, for having twenty-plus years' worth of conversations about our mysterious world and universe, and for tirelessly providing feedback on this book and all the others.

ABOUT THE AUTHOR

C.K. Kelly Martin is the author of such acclaimed young adult novels as *I Know It's Over*, *One Lonely Degree*, *The Lighter Side of Death*, *My Beating Teenage Heart*, *Yesterday*, *Tomorrow*, *The Sweetest Thing You Can Sing*, and *Delicate*. A graduate of the Film Studies program at York University, Martin currently resides in Oakville, Ontario. *Stricken* is her first book for middle-grade readers.